Deadly Clues

AMRITENDU MUKHERJEE

LAUNCHPAD

An imprint of
Srishti Publishers & Distributors

For every detective at heart—may you uncover secrets hidden in plain sight.

Srishti Publishers & Distributors
A unit of AJR Publishing LLP
212A, Peacock Lane
Shahpur Jat, New Delhi – 110 049

editorial@srishtipublishers.com

First Published by Launchpad,
an imprint of Srishti Publishers & Distributors in 2025

10 9 8 7 6 5 4 3 2 1

Contents

Where It All Began....................1

A Deadly Quest for Justice....................66

The Deadly Gambit....................88

What Lies Beyond....................112

One Eye, One Shot....................141

Acknowledgments....................189

Where It All Began

My classmate Kiran had seemed gloomy since morning. He wasn't talking to anyone at school.

I asked him during the lunch break, 'What's up? You don't seem like yourself today. Did you get a scolding at home?'

'Worse. My family is going through a nightmare.'

'What happened?'

'Not here,' Kiran lowered his voice. 'Let's meet in the games room during the off period. Mom told me not to tell anyone, but I'll tell you.'

We met in the games room during the break. It wasn't crowded. Two boys from different classes played table tennis while a girl threw darts. Her darts seemed to hit everywhere except the dartboard. We started playing chess to talk privately.

Kiran began, his voice barely audible, 'It started the day before yesterday. Mom suddenly screamed from the bathroom. We all rushed there and saw blood splattered on the wall—no idea where it came from.'

'My God!'

'That was just the beginning. My uncle, a zoologist, travels the world studying animals. He came back from a tour the day before yesterday. Yesterday afternoon, he went to the garden to water the plants. Suddenly, he returned and asked me to check the back of his kurta because he felt something wet. I shuddered when he turned around—there was blood spattered all over his back.

'Later, when Dad returned from work, it was already dark. He spotted a silhouette behind a tree at the far end of the garden. As Dad approached to investigate, someone threw blood at his face. Thankfully, his glasses saved his eyes, but he couldn't see who did it. The garden is dense with shrubs and trees—anyone can easily hide there. Everyone has been terrified ever since. None of us could sleep last night. God knows who's doing all this.'

'That sounds serious! Haven't you informed the police?' I asked sympathetically.

'Dad wanted to, but Grandpa disagreed. He has the final say in our family. Grandpa retired from a senior post in the Kolkata Police. He said, "I know what the cops in this city can and cannot do. They won't be able to solve this problem. Let's find a good private detective instead."'

'Detective?' I almost shouted.

The girl stopped throwing darts and turned to look at us. When she saw us hunched over the board, she lost interest and returned to her game. At least her darts were hitting the board now.

I lowered my voice, 'Are you seriously looking for a detective?'

'Yes, but it's difficult to find a good one these days. Most detectives only handle cases involving marriages and affairs. They wouldn't know how to deal with this.'

'I could ask my elder brother, Vik, to take a look—if your grandpa agrees.'

'What? Is he a detective?' Kiran looked puzzled.

'Not really,' I admitted. 'But he has remarkable observational and analytical skills. Like Sherlock Holmes, he can deduce many things about a person just by looking at them. And he wants to be a detective someday.'

'That's great,' Kiran finally smiled. 'I'll tell Grandpa. I'm sure he'll agree. Since our dads are friends, I don't think your dad will say no either.'

'Vik will be interested when I tell him about this. He's already told me he'll make me his assistant,' I felt a rush of excitement.

'Both of you should be awarded for what I'd call the worst game of chess I've ever seen,' said a voice beside me.

We looked up to see the school's chess champion staring at our board with a wide grin.

***

I sprinted home, my breath catching in excitement, only to be disappointed—Vik wasn't there. Mom, the figure of calm, told me he'd gone to the Mixed Martial Arts Club.

After a quick refreshment, I rushed to the club, which was within walking distance. An event was underway, and the place was packed. The guy at the gate, familiar with me from previous visits with Vik, let me in, though he gave me an odd look.

Inside, the atmosphere was electrifying. The large hall was dimly lit, with two spotlights focused on a fighting ring, now converted into a cage. The galleries were packed with a cheering crowd. I remembered Vik mentioning an inter-club championship scheduled at his club. Scanning the crowd, I searched for him but couldn't spot him. Assuming he was among the contestants, I sat in the gallery.

The compere's voice boomed, 'Welcome to the first inter-club MMA championship. Our club is proud to host this event. As you already know, we have a theme of masked MMA competitions. Contestants will wear masks, and the winner will reveal his face only at the end of each fight. So, let's welcome our first pair of contestants—the blue contestant, representing our club, The Fearless Warriors, and the red contestant, representing The Formidable Fight Club!'

The crowd erupted into applause as the contestants entered

the ring. The blue contestant resembled Vik, though his face was masked. From the back row, my view of the action was blurry at best. The blue contestant started strong, launching a relentless barrage of punches and kicks, forcing the red fighter to stumble under the pressure.

I knew Vik was an incredibly talented fighter. His teacher once insisted I learn MMA, saying, "Your brother has the talent to compete in the UFC one day. He's a world-class fighter. Surely, you have it in you, too. Come, train with us."

But now, he was not fighting like a world-class or even an amateur street fighter. He had started well, but the red guy was showing off his skills now. He performed a clinch, but Vik struggled to get out of it. At last, he managed to release himself, only to be taken down to the ground by the red fighter.

'What the hell is Vik doing?' I muttered under my breath.

'This is no place for kids,' a calm voice startled me.

I turned to see a man in a black hoodie seated beside me. His face was barely visible beneath the oversized hood.

'Vik, you're here! I thought you—'

'Fighting in the ring? Nope.' He shook his head. 'I didn't participate because of a shoulder injury. That's my friend, Akash. Not very talented but daring to a fault, often biting off more than he can chew. He always challenges fighters better than him. One day, it'll get him killed,' Vik sighed.

'Then why are you hiding your face?' I asked.

'Three people have already asked why I'm not participating. I'm tired of answering the same question, so I thought it best to keep a low profile. Anyway, what brings you here, Rik?'

My name is Ritwik Chatterjee, but everyone calls me Rik.

I replied, 'I have more interesting news than this fight.'

'Let's go upstairs then. There's a protein bar.'

As we headed upstairs, Akash, the blue fighter, was on the verge of defeat.

The protein bar on the first floor was a quieter spot. Vik removed his hoodie. 'Let me get us some protein shakes,' he said, walking to the counter.

Let me tell you a bit about my elder brother, Vik. His full name is Victor Chatterjee. He's twenty-three years old, nine years older than me, and in his final year of M.Sc. in chemistry. Vik stands at about 5'11', has an athletic build, and is fair-complexioned and undeniably handsome. He back-brushes his hair and prefers casual attire.

But what makes Vik truly remarkable are his sharp eyes, which seem to look straight into a person's soul. He doesn't study much, yet he's always the topper in his class, thanks to his excellent memory and intelligence. While most people his age party, drink and hang out with their girlfriends, Vik stays away from all that. Instead, he spends his time practising martial arts, reading his favourite books on forensic science and criminology, or developing new skills. His friends call him unsocial and dull, but I know better. Vik's analytical skills and keen observation make him fascinating.

Vik returned with two chocolate protein shakes. Then, pulling out his phone, he said, 'Before you share your interesting news, look at this. You didn't do your job properly.'

He showed me a screenshot of a news article I had sent him a week ago. I had been tasked with sending him screenshots of intriguing crime stories since he didn't like reading newspapers.

The headline read:

Poachers at Large in the Gir Forest

The Forest Department reported the disappearance of two fully grown lions from Gujarat's Gir Forest. The police officer on duty claimed they were investigating the matter but found no clues. The Chief Forest Officer blamed a group of active poachers in the area. The Police claim that the lions were hunted at night using silenced guns and then smuggled out. The state police have been on high alert since reports of several animals being hunted from nearby forests made the headlines. An officer from the department described it as 'a daring act'. The gang is said to have been using Rajasthan's border for smuggling. The Police Commissioner assured the public of safety at a press conference last night.

I said, 'I know. I sent this to you last week. Why are you telling me I didn't do my job properly?'

Vik scrolled further. 'You missed this one,' he said.

The headline read:

Poachers of Gir in Soup

Yesterday, the Gujarat police, in a feat of bravery, apprehended the elusive poacher gang, which is said to have hunted two lions and various other animals for commercial gains. The Police Commissioner announced the arrest of two gang members. According to the police, the suspects have provided vital information about the racket that will lead to many more arrests shortly. However, the gang leader remains unidentified and at large. The Commissioner is confident that the entire gang will be caught soon.

I had overlooked this report. Still, I tried to justify myself by saying, 'The police have already solved the case, so I didn't send it to you.'

'That was a mistake. Always follow up on cases,' Vik admonished. 'Now, scroll down and read this.'

The next headline was chilling:

Unknown Burnt Body in Bhalgaon

Last night, a burnt and unidentifiable body was found in a deserted field in Bhalgaon, Barmer. On questioning the villagers, it was found that the villagers had no clue how the body got there. Preliminary investigation revealed that the unidentified male victim was shot in the chest and killed before his body was burnt. Police officers present on the scene stated that the victim was killed elsewhere and his body dumped as the villagers did not hear any gunshot or screams the previous night. The body was discovered with no belongings apart from a metallic crucifix necklace. As of now, the identity of the deceased remains a mystery.

'Do you think this murder is related to the poacher gang?' Vik asked.

'That's a stretch,' I said sceptically.

'I know, but my gut tells me there's a connection. The village of Bhalgaon is on the India-Pakistan border and is also very close to Gujarat, and the smugglers were reportedly using Rajasthan's border.'

'Do you want to waste time chasing something far beyond your reach?' I snapped. 'Or hear about the case I brought you?'

Vik's demeanour changed. 'Really? A case? Are you serious?'

'One hundred per cent.'

'Then go on. What are you waiting for?'

As I recounted everything Kiran told me, Vik leaned forward, his sharp eyes fixed on mine, absorbing every detail with his trademark intensity. When I finished, he commented, 'Fascinating case, indeed. It seems someone is trying to intimidate Kiran's family. We'll need Dad's permission before getting involved, though. Let's hope Kiran's dad gives him a call. Now, let's head home, Rik. Don't you have to study?'

***

As we entered the house, we found Mum and Dad in the living room. Dad seemed to have just returned from work, as he hadn't changed yet. Both were seated with stern faces, making me feel a twinge of trepidation.

Mum stood up abruptly and rounded on me the moment I stepped inside. 'So, you think your brother is a great detective!'

My heart leapt. Kiran's dad must have already called.

Vik stood, his expression inscrutable.

Dad's tone was softer as he spoke, 'Sit down, boys. Let's discuss the matter.'

Mum scowled at him but said nothing. Instead, she turned and walked to the kitchen, muttering.

Dad watched her retreating figure with a sigh before turning back to us. 'My friend Rajen, your classmate's father'—Dad glanced at me—'called me a while ago. He asked for your help'—Dad gestured towards Vik—'in solving some mysterious incidents in his house. I suggested he go to the police or hire a professional detective, but he insisted you take a look first. It's his father's wish. Rajen assured me there's no danger involved, as his father is an ex-policeman with significant connections in the department. I reluctantly agreed. That's why your mum is furious with me.'

A jolt of excitement coursed through me. Vik couldn't suppress his delight either.

'Shall we go now?' he asked eagerly.

'We?' Dad asked darkly, his gaze shifting between Vik and me.

After a brief pause, he relented. 'Yes, I suppose. They're

expecting both of you. Unless you have homework to finish, Rik.'

'I don't have much homework. I can finish it after we return.'

I immediately regretted my words. Mum had returned from the kitchen and was glaring at me.

'Listen, you two,' she said scornfully. 'Since your dad couldn't say no to his friend, go there. Listen to what they say, and then you say no, Vik. I want no funny business. Tell them you can't do it and come back. Am I clear?'

Vik tried to pacify her. 'In that case, do we need to go at all, Mum? Dad could call Rajen Uncle and tell him we have studies.'

'No, Vik,' Dad interrupted as Mum opened her mouth to respond. 'You'll go. Rajen's dad has invited you both for snacks, and it would be rude to refuse.'

Mum didn't argue further. She turned and disappeared into the kitchen again.

'That settles it,' Vik said. 'Let's go, Rik. As you've heard, they're expecting us.'

We were back on the streets within five minutes. Vik took his bicycle, and I perched sidesaddle on the front.

As the cycle sped down the lane, I said, 'What if Kiran's grandpa wants to test your detective skills before letting you help? From what I've heard, he seems like a strict person.'

'I hope he doesn't ask me to deduce something about him. That would be so cliché,' scoffed Vik. 'Detective stories always sell this image of a good detective. He must be able to deduce everything about a person just by looking at them. I recently read a few novels by a contemporary writer who uses the pseudonym "Marichi". No exceptions.'

***

It took us about ten minutes to reach Kiran's house, a two-storey building with a garden. A pebbled path led up to the house from the main entrance, flanked by well-tended greenery on either side.

Kiran opened the door and ushered us in. The living room was spacious and well-decorated but empty. We placed our shoes on the shoe rack, the top of which was stacked with old newspapers and magazines. Kiran escorted us upstairs, pointing to a room, and he said, 'This is Grandpa's room. Please come in.'

The room exuded the ambience of an interview. All the family members were already present. Kiran's grandfather, Anshu Mondal, sat on his bed, facing the room's entrance. Though likely in his seventies, he had a toned physique, grey hair, and a thick moustache. A gentleman seated next to him appeared to be Kiran's zoologist uncle. Kiran's parents occupied a sofa to the side of the centre table. A servant stood quietly in one corner of the room.

We sat on the couch facing the bed, across the centre table. Kiran sat next to his grandfather, opposite his uncle. An empty sofa faced Kiran's parents.

After a few moments of pin-drop silence, Mr Mondal addressed Vik. 'I've heard about you from my grandson. I'd like to give you a job to do. But first, I need to confirm whether you're up to it. I'll ask you something. Are you ready to answer?'

'Yes, I think,' Vik replied with a shrug.

'Well then. A detective should be able to tell a few things about a person through observation. So, I want you to observe us and say whatever you can deduce.'

Vik glanced sidelong at me, an amused expression flickering across his face. He then looked at Rajen Uncle, Kiran's father, and said, 'I believe you're a cardiologist.'

Mr Mondal scoffed. 'That's too easy. You must've seen the nameplate outside the house.'

Rajen Uncle interjected, 'But I sent the nameplate for

painting. And I don't have a chamber in the house. So how could you tell?'

Even I was astonished. I'd never mentioned Kiran's parents' professions to Vik. I knew they were both doctors, but not their specialisations.

'Yes, you must explain how you deduced that,' Mr Mondal demanded, frowning. 'Guesswork won't do.'

'It's simple,' Vik began. 'I noticed a flyer on cardiac stents downstairs in the newspaper rack. These are usually handed out to doctors by company representatives, so I deduced that someone in the house is a cardiologist. Since I already knew the professions of the other inhabitants, it had to be either Uncle or Aunty. I was sure it was Uncle for two reasons. First, you have red marks on both sides of your neck, likely caused by contact dermatitis from hanging your stethoscope around your neck.'

Rajen Uncle rubbed his neck, nodding. 'You're right. It started after I got a new stethoscope. My dermatologist friend advised me to stop wearing it that way, but I just can't break the habit.'

'Impressive. And the second reason?' Mr Mondal asked.

'The second reason,' Vik continued, 'is that I deduced Aunty is a pathologist or an anatomist the moment I saw her.'

'You're right!' Krishna Aunty exclaimed, astonished. 'I am a pathologist. How did you know?'

'Firstly, the stains on your fingers. I noticed two colours: haematoxylin and eosin, which are commonly used by pathologists, microbiologists, and anatomists. As a chemistry student, I'm familiar with these stains. I assume you sometimes forget to wear gloves, which leads to stains. Secondly, upon entering this room, I detected a faint, pungent smell—the unmistakable scent of formalin. I'd encountered it before when visiting a pathologist friend's lab. I suspect you spilled some on your sari today.'

'You're right,' Krishna Aunty said, beaming.

I'd noticed the smell too but hadn't known it was formalin.

Everyone seemed impressed. Mr Mondal said, 'Very well. The final test—say something about me.'

Vik didn't respond immediately. Instead, he fiddled with his smartphone, studying Mr Mondal with amusement and curiosity. It was as if he'd figured something out and savoured the silence before delivering the revelation.

When he finally spoke, it was a bombshell. 'I believe, or rather, I'm quite certain, that you're the detective story writer who writes under the pseudonym "Marichi".'

The room fell into stunned silence. Even I was taken aback. Was Kiran's grandfather a writer?

Mr Mondal opened his mouth, clearly struggling to find words. 'I… I don't know how you could know that. No one outside this family is aware.'

'Quite obvious,' Vik replied smoothly. 'You have a prominent writer's callus on your right thumb and index finger, indicating you still write extensively despite being retired. Many retired police officers write crime stories based on their experiences, and I've read your books—they're largely procedural. Also, you've published only two books, but I noticed multiple copies of "Marichi's" books on your bookshelf. Writers often keep extra copies of their works. Furthermore, the bundle of printed papers with corrections on your desk is likely a proof copy of your next book. Lastly, "Anshu" and "Marichi" are both Sanskrit words meaning "sunrays".'

Mr Mondal looked overwhelmed, 'I have no doubt you're the right person for this job.'

The gentleman seated next to Mr Mondal spoke for the first time. 'Tell me something about myself too. Though I suppose I should introduce myself first.'

Mr Mondal nodded, 'Ah, yes. This is my younger son, Dhiren. Why should he be left out?'

Dhiren Uncle was a lean, clean-shaven man with a sober expression. He looked slightly pale, as though he might be unwell. His voice was soft, with noticeable pauses as he spoke.

Vik addressed him directly, 'I heard that you're a zoologist.'

Mr Mondal interjected, his tone proud, 'That's an understatement. He's a senior member of the World Wildlife Fund. We're all very proud of him.'

Dhiren Uncle looked embarrassed but didn't respond.

Vik continued, 'I believe you travelled to Rajasthan last week.'

Dhiren Uncle seemed startled for a fleeting moment, but he recovered quickly. 'No, I didn't. I was in Delhi last week,' he said calmly.

Vik frowned briefly but then smirked and turned to Mr Mondal, 'See? I can be wrong too. Perhaps you should reconsider whether I'm the right person for the job.'

Mr Mondal chuckled. 'Still, it was nearly correct. How did you arrive at that conclusion?'

'Let's skip the explanation,' Vik replied nonchalantly. 'After all, I was wrong.'

At that moment, the doorbell rang, and the servant left the room.

'The person I've been waiting for has finally arrived—late, as always,' Mr Mondal said.

A man, nearly as old as Mr Mondal, entered the room. He was fair and obese, wearing a dhoti and kurta, and carried an intricately carved wooden walking stick. He settled onto the empty sofa, pulling out a snuffbox from his pocket and taking a pinch of snuff with practised ease, which he did every little while as long as we were there.

'This is my friend, Shamick Acharya,' Mr Mondal introduced. 'He was once a formidable lawyer and is like family to us. I wanted him present for this discussion.'

After a brief pause, Mr Mondal turned to Vik, 'Did you hear what Kiran told your brother about the incidents at our house?'

Vik nodded.

'What do you make of all this?'

'I believe someone is trying to intimidate you. Who do you think would benefit from frightening you?'

'Quite right. This house has an expensive gem—a blue sapphire that has been in our family for generations. A week ago, a jeweller named Nirmal Bardhan came to our house and offered to buy it. He was willing to pay five lakhs, but I informed him it was worth at least ten times that amount. Regardless, I wasn't planning to sell it, as it is considered to bring fortune to our family. Before leaving, Bardhan told me that misfortune would follow if I didn't sell it. I inquired about him later and found out he has connections with smugglers. While I'm not certain he's behind the incidents, but his threats make him a prime suspect. That's why you're here. Find out who is behind this. Once you do, I'll inform the police and have them arrested. If you think this is too risky, feel free to decline. I'll handle it with the police in that case.'

Vik considered this for a moment before responding, 'Let me investigate. I'll let you know if I find it's beyond my control. But first, can I see the sapphire?'

'I expected you'd ask for that,' Mr Mondal said, pulling a small velvet box from his pocket.

Both Vik and I looked in awe as he opened it. Inside was a sapphire, the size of a grape, precisely cut to perfection. It gleamed with alternating red and blue hues. We held it in turn, marvelling at its beauty.

'Where is it kept?' Vik asked.

'In the prayer room on this floor. It's stored in a wooden box beside the Ma Laxmi idol. The box is always locked, as is the prayer room. I open both locks myself during morning prayers and keep the only keys. There are no duplicates. No one outside the family, except Shamick, knows where it's kept. Very few people even know of its existence. I can't fathom how Bardhan found out about it. I no longer feel it's safe to keep it here. I'm considering moving it to a bank locker.'

'Yes, that's a good idea. Please do it as soon as possible,' Vik advised.

'I have a bad feeling about this,' Mr Acharya muttered. 'Anshu, you should inform the police.'

'I'm firm on this, Shamick. Let's give this young man a chance. I believe he'll find a solution.'

Vik stood up, 'I'll take a look at the garden tomorrow morning. I promise to do my best.'

Mr Mondal asked Kiran to see us off, but Dhiren Uncle interjected, 'I'll accompany them, Kiran. It's already dark. You stay here.'

As we approached Vik's parked bicycle, Dhiren Uncle turned to Vik, 'Victor, I need to tell you something.'

Vik raised an eyebrow, 'First, tell me why you hid the truth.'

Both Dhiren Uncle and I froze in surprise.

Recovering quickly, Dhiren Uncle admitted, 'You're right. I did go to Rajasthan. I didn't want my father to worry about me. But let me be clear—these threats aren't connected to the blue sapphire. They're aimed at me, not Father.'

'Can you elaborate?' Vik asked.

Dhiren Uncle hesitated, visibly torn. 'I'm not sure whether I should. I don't want to put you in harm's way.'

Vik chuckled softly, 'From your body language, it's clear I'm already in harm's way just by coming here.'

Dhiren Uncle sighed, 'Very well. You already know what I do for a living. My work has put me in this position. For years, I've been investigating an illegal hunting gang that operates across India, Bangladesh, and Myanmar. I've coordinated with police and forest departments in these countries to arrest several members of the gang. Recently, this gang killed two lions in Gujarat. I received a tip that they were smuggling the lions through the Rajasthan border, so I went there last week. With my help, the police arrested two gang members, but we couldn't get any information about the gang leader.'

Vik nodded, 'We read about that case in the news.'

'Yes,' Dhiren Uncle continued. 'It happened the day before I returned to Kolkata. The police revealed the arrests later. That evening, I received a call from a journalist named Manmatha Sen. He told me he'd come to India from the UK to research an article on illegal hunting. He claimed to have cracked the case and knew who the gang leader was.

'I asked him for the name, but he refused to tell me over the phone. Instead, he asked me to meet him at a bar. I went at the specified time, but he didn't show up. As I was leaving, someone bumped into me. Later, in the taxi, I found a letter in my pocket.

'The letter said the bar was being watched and he couldn't meet me there. He asked me to return to Kolkata immediately, as it wasn't safe for me to stay in Rajasthan. He mentioned an address where I could meet him in Kolkata. Tomorrow morning, I plan to visit him.'

'Can I see the letter?' Vik asked.

'I destroyed it, as he instructed,' Dhiren Uncle replied.

'This sounds serious. Why haven't you informed the police?'

'Manmatha warned me not to. He said the gang leader has powerful connections, including moles within the police. That's why he's reaching out to me. But I don't understand why he didn't mention the leader's name in the letter or over the phone. I still have no concrete information, and it seems the gang is already after me. Perhaps they spotted me in the bar.'

'Or they're simply trying to scare you off,' Vik suggested. 'If they knew you had crucial information, they'd have done more than just threaten you.'

'What if they've already captured Manmatha?'

'I doubt it. If they had, they wouldn't bother trying to intimidate you. Still, you should assume your life is in danger. Why haven't you told your father? He influences the department.'

'I don't want to trouble him. He'd make a fuss and start calling everyone he knows, which would only draw attention to the situation. He's always been overprotective of me. That's why I'm telling you instead.'

'What do you want me to do?' Vik asked, intrigued.

'For now, nothing. I've already contacted the WWF. They're sending a team of Interpol members to assist me later this week. In the meantime, I need to meet Manmatha and gather as much information as possible. Here, take this.'

Dhiren Uncle handed Vik a slip of paper. 'This is the address mentioned in the letter. I suggest you don't go there alone—it's too risky. I'll handle this. But if anything happens to me, please give this to the police.'

'But you said the police might be compromised,' Vik pointed out.

'I know. But if the worst happens, it'll be the only option. Just promise me you won't take unnecessary risks. You're young and talented, Vik. Don't throw that away.'

Vik pocketed the paper without a word.

As we rode home, I broke the silence, 'What do you think, Vik?'

'I think we're in deeper waters than we realised,' he replied.

'I won't lie—I'm scared. This feels dangerous. And you mentioned we're already in harm's way.'

'Be brave, Rik. Investigations are rarely safe. If you want to be my assistant, you must prepare for greater threats.'

'But how did you know Dhiren Uncle had been to Rajasthan?'

Vik smiled faintly, 'You'd have figured it out if you'd been paying attention. On the newspaper rack downstairs, there was a copy of the Jaipur Times, dated four days ago. It's a local supplement distributed with The Times of India. Since we knew he'd returned recently, it was an obvious deduction.'

'Amazing. But if he wanted to hide his trip to Rajasthan, why leave the newspaper in the open?'

'He probably left it there absent-mindedly. You saw how stressed he looked.'

I nodded, 'So, what's next?'

'For now, we wait. As he said, I'm supposed to do nothing until the next incident.'

***

I could not have imagined that the next incident would be so devastating.

I woke up at 3 am the following day, hearing a commotion. The light in the living room was switched on. I heard Dad's anxious voice. I went there to find everyone awake and alarmed.

My voice trembled as I asked, 'What happened?'

Vik looked aghast, 'Terrible thing, Rik! Kiran's uncle has been murdered, and his body has disappeared.'

'What!' My heart pounded.

'Yes. Dad and I are going there now.'

'You are going? What about the cops?'

'On their way.'

Mum looked disgruntled, 'Why do you two have to poke your noses into this business? The police will do whatever needs to be done. There is danger….'

Dad stopped her, 'We have to. Rajen personally called and informed me. I must stand by his side in this dangerous time. Don't worry. We'll be fine. We'll be back in the morning.'

I whispered my wish to tag along into Vik's ear.

He whispered back, 'Don't be a fool. Do you want to face Mum's wrath? Tell her you are going to the playground early in the morning.'

I went to bed but couldn't sleep anymore. Thoughts rushed into my mind. Who could have killed Dhiren Uncle? How had his body disappeared? Did someone want to stop him from meeting Manmatha Sen? Had the journalist reached Kolkata? Was there any connection between these incidents and the blue sapphire?

The night seemed never-ending. Finally, I got up at 5 am and left home, telling Mum I was off to the playground. I reached Kiran's house, almost running.

A police car was parked outside. Two constables were posted at the gate. They stopped me.

'He is with me. Please let him enter,' I heard Vik's voice from the garden.

I found him behind a tree, looking at the ground with both hands on his waist.

'What are you doing here? Where is everyone?'

'Everyone is inside. Be careful, don't trample over the

footmarks,' Vik said, holding me by the arm as I tried to walk past him.

'All right,' I said, turning around. 'Can you tell me what happened last night? I was so anxious that I couldn't sleep.'

'Well. It happened at around 2 am. Kiran's parents were sleeping in their room on the ground floor. Both woke up hearing screams from the garden. They found the front door open as they came out to investigate the source. They faced a horrid scene while entering the garden. Mr Dhiren was lying down with a knife stabbed to the hilt on the left side of his chest. He was panting for his last breath but still alive.'

'My God, did Rajen Uncle pull the knife out? He is a doctor, after all.'

'Ridiculous! Think, Rik. No doctor would do such a thing and risk accelerating the blood loss. He told Krishna Aunty to stay with Dhiren Uncle and rushed into the house to call an ambulance. When he came back, Dhiren Uncle had disappeared. Aunty was lying unconscious on the ground. Mr Mondal and the servant, Ravi, had come out by then. But everything happened so quickly. Rajen Uncle said he saw a car speeding away towards the south of the road at the left side of the house when he came out the second time. There is a postern door on the left side of the garden. Probably Dhiren Uncle had been carried away through that door. Krishna Aunty regained consciousness in a few minutes. She said as soon as her husband left, someone's arm wrapped around her neck from behind. She had felt dizzy immediately and blacked out within a few seconds. She was likely held in a carotid headlock, cutting off blood flow to her brain. But just before passing out, she saw Dhiren Uncle going limp.'

'Horrible! How ruthless these assailants are!' I exclaimed. 'But why did you tell me that Dhiren Uncle was murdered? No one ever saw his corpse. So, he may still be alive, right!'

'Impossible! No one can survive such a deep stab into the heart. The assailants were professionals. Rajen Uncle confirmed that the knife was positioned in such a manner that it would surely have gone into the heart. Even if he had been taken to the hospital, he had almost zero chances of survival. I hope you know that the heart is on our chest's left side.'

'Terrible!' I felt a lump in my throat, the weight of the situation pressing down on me. I hadn't even imagined such a ghastly fate awaited him when we talked to him in the same garden yesterday evening.

After a brief silence, I asked, 'But what were you doing in the garden? Were you searching for clues? Did you find any?'

Vik grinned as if he had been waiting for this question. 'Let me show you.'

We came to the west side of the garden. Here the lawn was laid bare. Due to the occasional rainfall in the past few days, the soil was wet. I noticed a large puddle of dark brown gooey material on the ground. There was no doubt that it was clotted blood. My stomach lurched.

Vik pointed to that and said excitedly, 'Dhiren Uncle was lying here. But look, how much he was bleeding! Much blood, indeed!'

I felt nauseated. Who feels such devilish pleasure at the sight of blood? Was Vik out of his mind?

Vik continued, 'Look closely. The ground is a mess of footprints, but the police didn't pay them much attention. So, they trampled all over the place. Yet, I studied them carefully and found some important clues. Look at these signature footmarks of police boots. We can ignore them. Now, there are a few footprints of slippers. These are probably of the inhabitants of the house, including Dhiren Uncle himself. Apart from these are footprints of at least two outsiders, both wearing sneakers. I believe they were hiding somewhere nearby, probably there.'

Vik pointed to a tamarisk tree. We went there.

Vik said in a disappointed tone, 'This area is grassy. No footprint here.'

I bent down and picked up a cigarette butt.

Vik snatched it from my hand and said, 'So we have solid proof that outsiders were lurking in the garden. I don't think anyone in this house is a smoker.'

We came back to the spot where Dhiren Uncle was last seen.

Vik continued, 'Notice how the two sets of footprints lead towards the postern door. Do you see anything odd about them?'

I observed them for some time but couldn't find anything unusual.

Vik scoffed, 'You have such a long way to go, Rik. Can't you even pick up the simple clue that these footmarks were facing each other? So that means one of the guys walked forward and the other walked backwards from here. Now, what does that mean to you?'

I mumbled, 'Maybe after killing Dhiren Uncle, they turned against each other. One guy was advancing to attack while the other backed away?'

Vik looked incredulous, 'That's your interpretation? I must say, it's rather naive and overly imaginative. My dear, this means that those two guys carried Dhiren Uncle towards the postern door. Look carefully. There are occasional drops of blood on the soil. That's how he disappeared. But we don't know whether he was still alive.'

I asked the question that had been bothering me for some time. 'But why did they take him away? They had already delivered the fatal blow, as you said. What else did they hope to achieve by making the body disappear?'

'Excellent question. At last, you are talking sensibly now,' Vik patted my back. 'Unfortunately, it is also the most difficult question to answer. There can be several possibilities. Some criminals hide or dump the body to destroy evidence. Some also do that to misdirect the investigation. But that doesn't seem to be the situation here. We need to keep in mind that Dhiren Uncle was still alive. Though Kiran's mother had seen him going limp, he could have just passed out. The criminals knew that the house's inhabitants had already been alerted and there was not enough time to finish the job. Sometimes a person can breathe up to a few hours even after receiving a fatal blow. And the dying man could reveal information that could put them in trouble. So, they carried him away to ensure that he couldn't say anything to anyone before dying. Another possibility is that he was rescued by someone else, either Manmatha or the Interpol team who were not yet ready to reveal themselves. And the least possible chance is that Dhiren Uncle survived by some miracle and is now hiding from the criminals. Keep your mind open, Rik. Let's go out and check where the getaway vehicle was waiting.'

We went out of the garden through the postern door. A concrete road stretched there, joining the main roads at the front and back of the house. According to Rajen Uncle, the car fled towards the south, the backside of the house.

Vik pointed to the road and said, 'Look at the chunk of soil here and the tyre marks. There was rainfall just past midnight, and the car must have crossed a muddy road. Ahh… what's that?'

Vik went back towards the door and picked up another cigarette butt.

'Same brand,' he muttered.

'This means that the man waiting behind the tamarisk tree

was sitting in the car first when he smoked this one,' I suggested. 'Or is this the second man? As you said, two men carried Dhiren Uncle away.'

'It is not necessary that both of them smoked. And it also does not have to be the same person, as two guys can share cigarettes from the same packet. I believe it is the driver of the car, the third guy.'

'How can you be sure there was a third guy?'

'I am not sure; I am just guessing. Usually, you need three people for such an operation, two for the job and one getaway driver. So, it seems more logical that there were at least three, if not four. Let's go back. There is nothing to see here.'

We returned to the garden, retracing our steps through the chaotic scene.

I asked Vik, 'Aren't the cops bothered that you are meddling with their investigation? I am surprised that they allow you to roam freely in the crime scene.'

Vik chuckled, 'That is the tricky part. You'll see for yourself in a while. But, first, let's go inside.'

***

The inspector, Mr Asit Sarkar, was an amiable middle-aged gentleman. He was of average height, dark-complexioned, and stout, with the hint of a paunch.

He addressed Vik, 'Hi, how is it going? Found anything worth telling apart from those useless theories about footprints, Mr Victor Holmes?' He seemed amused at his joke. 'And who have you brought along this time? Young Watson?'

I felt irritated.

Vik shook his head calmly, 'Nothing new. I have already told you whatever I have learnt. This is my brother, Ritwik.'

Inspector Sarkar gave a guffaw and declared, 'Consider yourself lucky that I am allowing you to roam freely. Anshu sir was my mentor, and I cannot say no to his wishes to this day. But let him learn the hard way that the police cannot be replaced by a novice detective who doesn't even have a licence. I could have refused his demand and made you sit in the room with the others. But I have learned a lot from Anshu sir and didn't want to disrespect him on the day that he lost his son. So, I am allowing you to look around. But should you hinder this investigation in any way or withhold information from me, your clearance will be revoked.'

'I am aware of that, Officer,' Vik replied.

'Now, I am going to search Mr Dhiren's room. You can tag along if you want to learn some real detective work. Come, Watson!' Inspector Sarkar patted my back with a smirk on his face.

Dhiren Uncle's room was next to Mr Mondal's. Mr Mondal's door was open, but the curtains were drawn. So, I couldn't see who was sitting inside. Dhiren Uncle's room was smaller. It was neat and clean. The furniture included a single bed, wardrobe, bookshelf, study table with a drawer, and chair. The smaller items were a vintage wall clock, table clock, an emergency lamp, and a paper holder hung in one corner. There were numerous papers and books on the table. The bookshelf was also full of books, mostly on zoology. There were a few fiction books as well, including detective stories. A kitbag and a backpack sat in one corner of the floor. A picture of Tagore hung on the wall.

The police began searching the room painstakingly. Vik and I stood out of their way. I was looking around. A beige-coloured envelope lying on the study table soon drew my attention. Vik had also noticed it. He picked it up and found a white paper inside. He glanced at it and said, 'I think you are searching for this, Inspector Sarkar.'

Inspector Sarkar snatched the paper from Vik, looked at it once, and said, 'I see.'

I sneaked a peek and read it. There were only two lines written, probably with a black gel pen:

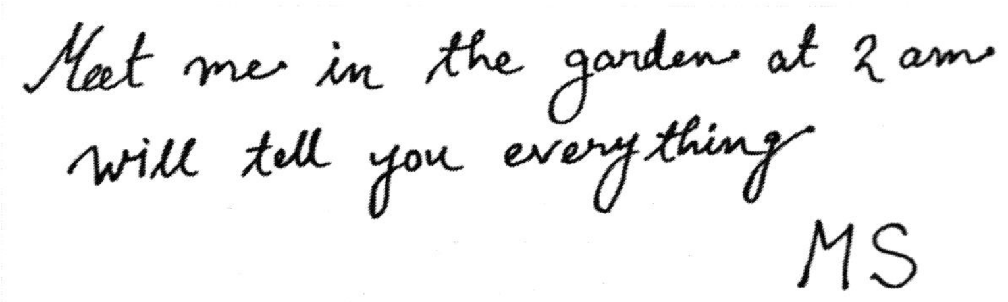
Meet me in the garden at 2 am
will tell you everything
MS

'That is why he went to the garden in the middle of the night,' Inspector Sarkar said. 'But who is MS?'

'Probably the initials for Manmatha Sen, the journalist I told you about,' Vik replied.

'Does that mean the poacher gang lured Dhiren Uncle into the garden by writing this fake letter?' I asked.

'Could be,' Vik shrugged.

Inspector Sarkar said smugly, 'That's what happens when you play detective instead of letting the police do their job. I hope you have understood that, Mr Chatterjee.'

'I understood that someone delivered this letter personally in hand or dropped it in the mailbox as there is no postage stamp on the envelope. Whoever wrote this initially tried to hide his original handwriting but eventually failed. And finally, the writer took dictation from someone else.'

'What! The postage stamp thing is clear. But how can you say the other things?' Inspector Sarkar was taken aback. I was also surprised.

Vik took the letter and pointed, 'Look at the "M". The first looks rather forcefully decorated and excessively slanted, while the one in "MS" looks different. Also, look at the "e". The initial few, particularly the first two, look shaky and different. But the last ones look more uniform. That means the writer initially intended to mask his original handwriting but later gave it up as a bad job and returned to his original handwriting.'

'And how can you say that it was dictated?' I asked.

'That is rather simple. Whenever we take dictations, we have to stop until the person dictating says the next word. The writer of this letter stopped four times. That is quite obvious as the pen wasn't lifted from the paper while awaiting dictation, and the ink from the gel pen created dots at those places. The writer stopped after writing "me", "garden", "am", and "everything". Check carefully.'

Vik had dropped an atomic bomb. Inspector Sarkar looked dumbfounded. The two constables searching the room made awkward faces as they were impressed but couldn't express themselves in front of their OC. I was wickedly delighted at the officer's setback, as he had been behaving quite irritably.

I said, 'I have a hunch. The gang leader must have dictated this letter to MS himself. There is a possibility that MS joined hands with the gang after being offered much money. Otherwise, Dhiren Uncle wouldn't have gone to the garden.'

'Why?' Vik frowned at my inference.

'Because Dhiren Uncle knew MS's handwriting. How can you forget that MS had written a letter to him before?' I felt confident.

'Fascinating theory, Rik,' Vik chuckled. 'But probably, he wouldn't have remembered the handwriting, given his stress. It would have been easier for us if he hadn't burnt the letter.'

Inspector Sarkar declared, 'Nothing else to see here. Let's go.' He and the constables left the room, but Vik kept standing.

I asked, 'Do you want to search any further?'

Vik nodded. He started going through the papers on the table. Then he went to the bookshelf, took a few books, and casually flipped through the pages. Next, he took the paper holder in his hand and said, 'This paper holder reminds me of a story. Have you read *The Purloined Letter* by Edgar Allan Poe?'

I shook my head.

'You should. The story tells us how things can be hidden in plain sight. The antagonist of the story stole an important letter. The police searched everywhere in his house, including under the carpets and behind the wallpapers. But the letter was nowhere to be found. Finally, the detective found it in a cheap card rack hung from the wall. It had always been there in front of everyone, but nobody had bothered to look at it.'

'Have you found something like that hidden in this paper holder?' I asked.

'Nope,' Vik shook his head. 'Though these cash memos look out of place. Have a look at the first five memos.'

Vik handed me the paper holder. I didn't find anything odd in those cash memos. It seemed that Dhiren Uncle was a frequenter of the College Street book market and used to purchase many books. These five cash memos from five different shops listed forty-five books. Total expenditure was approximately six thousand rupees. The book names were written in unrecognisable handwriting in all memos, although I could figure out the words "communication," "media," and "public". Only one of the memos was dated—the day before yesterday, the day Dhiren Uncle returned from the tour.

'He was quite a book lover,' I commented while placing the paper holder back in its place. 'He visited the book market the day he returned from the tour. But why did you say that these cash memos are out of place? Dhiren Uncle was surely a bookworm. His bookshelf proves that.'

'I am not saying that he didn't like books. But would you fancy visiting the book market when your life is in danger?'

'He had visited the market probably before the threatening and blood splatter began,' I shrugged.

We came to Mr Mondal's room where all the family members, Mr Shamick, and Dad sat. Dad was astonished to see me there but didn't say anything. There was an air of grief hanging in the room.

Mr Shamick suddenly asked the question that had bothered me for some time, 'Anshu, is the sapphire safe?'

Mr Mondal sighed, 'I don't care anymore, Shamick.'

'Still, it is better to check on it.'

'Okay. The key is there,' Mr Mondal pointed to the drawer. He then covered his face with his hands and assumed a stooping position. He seemed devastated.

Mr Shamick took the key and left the room.

Inspector Sarkar entered and addressed Mr Mondal, 'Sir, our preliminary investigation is over. I believe that the poacher gang is responsible for this. I beg your pardon, Sir, but had you called us earlier, this disaster could have been averted.'

Mr Mondal didn't reply. There was pin-drop silence in the room for a while, which was suddenly shattered by a scream from Mr Shamick. The inspector was going to say something, but he froze, with his mouth open.

'Gone! It is gone, Anshu!' Mr Shamick burst into the room, screaming, 'The stone is missing.'

'What!' Inspector Sarkar rushed out of the room. Everyone, even Vik, was startled. Only Mr Mondal was unaffected. He remained in the same stooping position.

Mr Shamick looked flustered as he continued, 'When I entered the prayer room, I found that the wooden box had been unlocked though the lid was closed. As I opened the lid, I found that the sapphire was missing. The small velvet box was lying wide open.'

Inspector Sarkar returned after five minutes and said, 'There can be only one explanation. Someone took advantage of the chaos and stole it. And I have a pretty good idea who may have done it.'

Mr Mondal said, 'I know you are trying to blame my servant, Ravi. He is very loyal. I don't want him harassed. So, I'll not file any case for the missing sapphire.'

'In that case, I can't take responsibility for finding it, Sir,' Inspector Sarkar shrugged.

'Don't worry about that, Asit. Instead, try to bring Dhiren's killers to justice. That's all I want.'

'Very well, then,' Inspector Sarkar left the room.

Vik asked, 'Where is the prayer room?'

Krishna Aunty replied, 'The last room at the end of the corridor.'

'Let's go and have a look, Rik.'

Mr Shamick had left the prayer room unlocked. It was a small room. The box was lying in front of the altar. It was a foot long and half a foot wide, polished and emblazoned wooden box. The empty small velvet box we had seen yesterday was lying in it. There were other ornaments in the chest; they were probably used to decorate the idols. Those did not seem to be expensive. The thief hadn't touched them.

Vik looked around for a minute. Then he walked towards the window, his eyes fixed on the windowsill. Traces of some brown powder were lying there. Vik took them on his fingertip and smelled them. He then turned towards me and said, 'I am done here. Let's go.'

I was baffled at his nonchalant expression. How could he be so calm after what had been happening since last night?

We went back to Mr Mondal's room. I consoled Kiran for a couple of minutes. He was pretty upset.

After spending another ten minutes, Dad stood up and said, 'I'll leave now. Don't hesitate to call me, Rajen, if you need anything. Come along, Vik and Rik.'

Mr Shamick also bade adieu to Mr Anshu.

Vik, who had been walking around with an air of confidence so far, messed up badly while going out. He tripped on the staircase. Had Mr Shamick not gotten hold of him in the nick of time, he would have broken a few bones.

Inspector Sarkar, still in the living room, scoffed, 'Are you having an attack of vertigo? You have probably realised this is too much for an amateur detective.'

Vik took a paper from his trouser pocket and handed it over to Mr Sarkar, 'Actually, I got absent-minded by a sudden realisation that I had forgotten to give you something important. This is the journalist's address. Manmatha Sen. Dhiren Uncle gave it to me yesterday.'

'Oh, I see. Go home safely. I'll not investigate the missing sapphire as Anshu sir has not filed a case. I won't mind if you try to find it. I can give you a heads-up, however. Don't trust this servant. Loyalty can easily be sold nowadays,' Inspector Sarkar grinned.

Vik returned a warm smile.

***

After returning from school, I found Vik in our living room, lost in deep thought. It was clear he had skipped college today. When I asked if he had found a solution, he simply shook his head.

I tried again, 'Any update from Inspector Sarkar? Though I

doubt he'd be interested in sharing much with you.'

'I called him. The blood collected from the crime scene matches Dhiren Uncle's blood group. They've sent it for a DNA test as a routine, but needless to say, it'll match.'

Leaving Vik to his thoughts, I went to freshen up.

Over evening tea, he finally said, 'Let's return to Dhiren Uncle's room, Rik. I have a gut feeling we missed something.'

On the way to Kiran's house, he added, 'This case is a tangled mess—illegal hunting, the suspicious journalist, threatening blood splatter, the lethal attack on Dhiren Mondal, and finally, the abduction of a dying man.'

I replied, 'To top it all, the missing sapphire.'

Vik blew a raspberry, 'Focus on the people, Rik, not the stone.'

***

As soon as we arrived, we went directly to Dhiren Uncle's room after asking for permission from Krishna Aunty.

Vik said, 'Keep your eyes open, Rik. Even a small piece of paper could be an important clue for us. Let me know if you find anything unusual.'

He started going through the papers on the table again. Meanwhile, I scanned the room, hoping to spot something useful. My attention was soon caught by a small envelope lying on the floor under the table. It was the kind of envelope photo studios usually use to deliver passport-size photographs. I picked it up. It was from Nayan Studio, but the envelope was empty. Instead, a number was written on it.

Vik took it from me and said, 'This studio is in Behala. Let's check it out. Though, if it turns out that Dhiren Uncle just clicked some photos for official work, it won't be of much use.'

'Anything else?' I asked, eager to help.

'Nah, Rik. Nothing,' Vik sighed. 'Let's head out.'

Neither Rajen Uncle nor Mr Mondal seemed to have any idea about the envelope from Nayan Studio.

As we were leaving the house, we ran into Mr Shamick.

'Hi, Mr Detective! Did you find any clues?' he asked airily.

I started, 'Yes, an envel—ouch.'

Vik had pinched me in the back.

'You must have been bitten by an ant, Rik,' he said quickly. 'I told you not to walk on the grass.'

Then, turning to Mr Shamick, he said, 'You must have heard about the envelope with the letter asking Dhiren Uncle to come to the garden.'

Mr Shamick looked puzzled. 'Yes, the inspector showed us a letter. But unfortunately, none of us could recognise the handwriting.'

As we walked away, I saw Mr Shamick staring at us, looking confused.

Once we were out of earshot, Vik scolded me. 'You were about to spill the beans. If you want to be a detective's assistant, learn to keep secrets.'

I bit my lip as Vik took out his phone.

'Where are we going?' I asked.

'Behala first, then Loudon Street.'

'What's in Loudon Street?'

'Manmatha Sen's house—the address Dhiren Uncle gave me.'

***

Nayan Studio was located off the main road in a quiet

neighbourhood. It was a small shop with a single person behind the reception desk.

Vik showed him the envelope and asked, 'Can you find the photo from this number? My friend used up all the copies and needs more.'

The shopkeeper took the envelope and said, 'Sure, give me a minute. We keep backups of all the photos.'

After a few clicks on his computer, the man paused and asked with curiosity, 'This doesn't look like you. Are you related to the person in the photo?'

'Yes,' Vik replied smoothly. 'My friend couldn't make it. I live nearby, so I offered to collect it.'

'All right. Let me print it—minimum six copies.'

'Sure,' Vik reached for his wallet. 'Also, send a high-resolution digital copy to my friend's email. This is the email ID. I don't want to return here just to get more prints.'

'Makes sense. By the way,' the man added, glancing at the screen, 'I see your friend had his photo taken only a month ago. Must be applying to many places or travelling a lot.'

Vik and I exchanged a glance but didn't reply.

When the shopkeeper handed over the photos, I half-expected to see Dhiren Uncle's face. But to my utter astonishment, the photo was of someone else—a middle-aged man with wheat-coloured skin, thick curly grey hair, and a prominent moustache. His most striking feature, however, was his green eyes.

'Who is this man? He doesn't even look Indian,' I said as we stepped out of the shop.

Vik examined the photo again. 'How would I know? It's odd, though. How did Dhiren Uncle end up with this picture?'

'Could this man be the leader of the poacher gang?' I ventured.

Vik frowned, 'Do you think the leader of a poacher gang

would walk into Nayan Studio for a photoshoot? That seems unlikely, don't you think?'

'Why not?' I argued. 'I've heard that many criminal and terrorist organisations use Kolkata as their base because of its proximity to the border.'

Vik considered this, 'Good point. Dhiren Uncle did say this gang operates in India, Bangladesh, and Myanmar. Kolkata would be a strategic location for their activities. But that still doesn't explain how Dhiren Uncle got this photo. He claimed he didn't know the gang leader's identity.'

I reminded Vik, 'He did say he'd been collecting evidence against this gang for some time. Maybe he found the photo but couldn't identify who this person was.'

'Possible,' Vik admitted. 'But you seem confident that this is the gang leader.'

'Just a gut feeling,' I said as I opened the door of the cab waiting for us.

***

It was almost dark when the cab dropped us at Loudon Street. During the ride, Vik had been engrossed in his mobile phone, barely saying a word. Manmatha Sen's house was easy to locate. Lined with single and two-storied houses, the neighbourhood was relatively quiet and exuded an air of affluence. It was also the kind of place where people minded their own business and paid little attention to their neighbours.

Our destination was a single-storied garden house. After ringing the doorbell several times, the door creaked open to reveal an elderly man. He was short, dark-complexioned, and dressed in a kurta and lungi. His expression was far from welcoming.

'What do you want?' he asked curtly.

'We're here to meet Manmatha Sen,' Vik said.

'He is not in the house.'

'When will he return?'

'No idea. Sorry, I'm busy. You may leave,' He moved to close the door.

But he couldn't.

My heart skipped a beat when I saw Vik's foot blocking the door. The man's glare turned sharper.

'What's the meaning of this?' the man demanded.

'I have a few questions,' Vik said evenly. 'I'm not leaving until you answer them.' He gave the door a firm push and stepped inside. I followed him, trying to mask my nervousness. The man grudgingly stepped back, allowing us entry.

The living room was dimly lit and sparsely furnished, with a sofa set and a centre table. A half-filled bookshelf stood against one wall, holding books on journalism. At one corner of the room was a small prayer area, complete with idols of Lakshmi-Narayana. However, what drew my attention was the stuffed head of a cheetah mounted on the wall. Vik's eyes lingered on it briefly too.

'I'll call the police,' the man growled.

'We're here on behalf of the police,' Vik replied smoothly. 'Calling them won't help you.'

'Since when has the police started hiring children?' he retorted with a sneer.

Vik's gaze hardened, 'You talk far too much for a mere servant. I'm beginning to doubt whether you are one.'

The man's face darkened. 'What do you mean? I am the caretaker of this house.'

'Very well then,' Vik said authoritatively. 'Let's make this easy. Answer my questions, and I'll leave. Sounds simple?'

'But I've already answered many questions for Inspector Sarkar this morning. They even searched the house.'

'Consider this the second round,' Vik said with a faint smile. 'What's your name?'

'Ratan.'

'How long have you been working here?'

'One year.'

'And how long has Mr Sen been residing here?'

'I don't know. There was another caretaker before me.'

'He seems to travel a lot.'

'Yes, he often travels to London and other places. I keep the house habitable.'

'Does Mr Sen own this house?'

'No idea.'

'Does anyone visit him here?'

'Yes, a few friends come often. Mr Vinod, Mr Pramanick, and Mr Ahuja. They come for meetings.'

'Meetings?' Vik raised an eyebrow. 'What do they discuss? Have you overheard anything?'

'Not much. I stay busy with my household chores. But I've caught bits and pieces while serving tea and snacks.'

'Anything noteworthy?'

Ratan hesitated, 'Once, about a month ago, they were talking about automatic rifles. I found that unusual.'

A chill ran down my spine.

'Did they discuss wild animals?' Vik asked.

Ratan shook his head, 'Not that I recall.'

Vik stepped toward a photo frame on the wall. It was a photograph of a man standing before Big Ben, holding a bulky camera. The man was young, fair, and handsome, dressed in a tee and jeans.

'Is this Mr Sen?' Vik asked.

'Yes.'

Vik turned to the bookshelf, scanning the spines of the books. Then he gestured toward the prayer area, 'Are these idols regularly worshipped?'

'No,' Ratan replied. 'I change the garlands daily and light a lamp every evening. Whenever Sir is home, he worships himself.'

Growing impatient, I asked, 'Has any foreigner ever come to meet your Sir?'

Ratan looked startled by my sudden question. He hesitated before replying, 'A foreigner?'

Vik took out one of the photos we'd just printed and showed it to him, 'Have you ever seen this man here?'

For a fleeting moment, Ratan's face seemed to stiffen. But he quickly recovered and replied casually, 'Nope. Never seen him before.'

After a brief pause, he added, 'You can leave your contact number. I'll call you if I remember anything.'

'That won't be necessary, we're done here. Let's go, Rik.' Vik said curtly, striding towards the door without another glance.

***

We were back on the street in a minute, now totally deserted.

Vik said, 'We must walk up to the junction to find a taxi. Let's walk fast, Rik. I don't want to linger in this neighbourhood.'

'What do you think, Vik?' I asked, speeding up. 'I don't trust this journalist anymore. He's surely involved in this whole affair.'

'Possibly,' Vik said absently. 'I'm unsure whether I made a mistake showing him that picture. But tell me, why do you think Manmatha is involved?'

'Didn't you listen to what Ratan said? He's hosted shady meetings in his house discussing firearms,' Again, I felt frustrated at Vik's lack of concern.

Vik scoffed, 'Didn't it occur to you that Ratan may have lied? You saw how he was acting over-smart. Honestly, though, I found nothing in that room to suspect Manmatha. And don't even talk about that cheetah head.'

'But I had this ominous feeling that I was in the enemy's den. Call it my gut feeling.'

'You're relying too much on gut feeling. Now, let's see if you've observed anything. Tell me what you saw in that room. Anything unusual?'

I shrugged, 'Seating area, bookshelf, prayer area—nothing unusual. Rather mundane. Nothing was interesting in the room except that cheetah head on the wall. The bookshelf contained only books on journalism, not even a single storybook. He must be a boring person.'

'Good,' Vik patted my shoulder. 'How many books were there on that bookshelf?'

'Are you for real?' I looked at Vik sceptically. 'You mean to say that you even cou…uuuuuu….' My words ended in a shriek as a bike zoomed past us and stopped with a screech, blocking our path.

Two men sat on the bike; their faces hidden under helmets. Both wore jeans and tees. The man at the rear held something shiny in his right hand, aimed at us. My stomach dropped as I realised it was a pistol.

'Turn out your pockets. No sudden movements if you want to live,' the man with the gun said in a husky voice.

I froze. Vik, however, remained calm as he took out his wallet and phone and handed them over to the armed man. The assailant checked the wallet and bellowed, 'Where is that envelope with photos?'

'Ah, you want that? Why didn't you say so before?' Vik asked, sounding almost amused.

The man brandished his gun. 'Don't act smart. Hand me the envelope, or I'll shoot you.'

'Sure.' Vik took the envelope from his back pocket.

'Take it.'

Vik stretched out his arm and dropped the envelope before the assailant could grab it. For a fleeting moment, the man's eyes darted downwards—as did the muzzle of his gun. Before he could react, Vik delivered two lightning-quick roundhouse kicks. The first sent the weapon flying several feet away, and the second struck his head. The man fell from the bike, his helmet skidding off.

Before the other man could react, Vik aimed an open-palm strike at him. However, he proved to be a better fighter than his companion. He stepped back and swung his leg in a counterattack, forcing Vik to retreat. Then, leaping over the bike, he launched a flurry of punches. Vik blocked them like a seasoned fighter and countered with a knee strike.

Meanwhile, the first assailant began to recover, staggering to his feet. Alarmed, I ran towards the edge of the road where the gun had landed, frantically searching. I found it soon. It was a 9 mm CZ75 handgun. My fingers trembled as they closed around the cold steel of the pistol, its weight unfamiliar yet oddly empowering. As I turned back, I saw the first man charging towards Vik, helmet in hand, while Vik was still locked in combat with the other assailant.

Realising the danger, I shouted, 'Vik, watch your back!'

Vik turned just in time to raise his arm in defence, but it wasn't enough. The helmet struck him squarely in the chest, sending him staggering back to the ground, winded.

The attacker raised the helmet again, but I shouted, 'Hands up!'

He turned to me, saw the pistol in my hands, and smirked,

'It's not a toy for kids. Hand it over, boy.' He took a step forward.

I cocked the gun, pointed it at him, and said, 'Try me.'

The smirk vanished, replaced by alarm as he realised I knew how to handle the weapon. Still, he quickly picked up the envelope and Vik's phone, shouting at his companion, 'Let's go!'

The other man, still groggy from Vik's attack, managed to lift the bike.

I shouted, 'Don't move or I'll shoot.'

They didn't heed my warning, so they got on the bike and sped off in the direction that they had come from. The assailants must have guessed I wouldn't dare to shoot, despite knowing how to handle the gun. That action required much more than the mere knowledge of firearms.

They were mistaken. I aimed the gun at the tyre of the speeding bike and pulled the trigger. But the CZ did not fire, leaving me helpless and furious.

'You need to take the safety off before firing,' Vik said, getting to his feet and clutching his chest. 'But you amazed me. How did you learn to cock a gun like that?'

'YouTube videos, of course,' I replied. 'I've watched plenty of shooting tutorials.'

Vik picked up his wallet, which the attackers had left behind, and said, 'Let's get to the main road. We're still not safe.'

As we rushed towards the junction, I replayed the events in my mind, and the answer was obvious. 'This must be Ratan's doing. He must have alerted his accomplices when we stepped out of the house. How else would they know about the envelope? I'm sure now that the man in the photo is the leader of the poacher gang.'

'Could be. But others also know about the envelope. We showed it to Mr Mondal and Rajen Uncle. The guy at the photo studio knows about it. Even Mr Shamick might have suspected something, considering you nearly spilt the beans. But credit goes to you for finding it.'

'What's the use?' I muttered, throwing my hands up in exasperation. 'They took it and your phone. We're back to square one.'

'Not before I sent the photo to Inspector Sarkar on WhatsApp. Plus, it's in my email inbox. The studio guy mailed it to me, remember?'

'They have your phone. They can delete it from your inbox. And if they see you've sent the photo to the police, they'll be alerted.'

'True. But I doubt they'll unlock my phone easily. Regardless, they'll be on high alert now, so we need to act fast.'

'What's the plan? Where are we going?'

We had reached the junction. Vik flagged down a yellow Ambassador taxi and announced as we climbed in, 'New Alipore police station.'

***

Inspector Sarkar was not at all happy to see us. Vik told him everything that had happened in the evening, and I handed over the handgun we had taken from the attackers.

'You shouldn't have gone to Manmatha's house. Look at the mess you've landed yourselves in. Had Anshu Mondal Sir not forbidden me to take any action against you, I'd have put both of you under house arrest until this case is solved,' Sarkar said, scowling at us.

'I was just trying to help. Have you seen the photo I sent you?' Vik asked.

'Yes, but finding a person based on only a photograph is difficult. There's an international passport database, but searching there will be like looking for a needle in a haystack. Billions of photographs are on that server. It could take hours, or even days, to find a match.'

'I don't think we have that kind of time,' Vik grunted.

'We! You think we're a team already?' Inspector Sarkar scoffed.

'I don't want any credit for capturing the gang. This is a great opportunity to learn from you, thanks to Anshu Sir, and I don't want to waste it.'

The flattery worked. Inspector Sarkar looked smug as he said, 'I agree you've made a significant discovery. The photograph seems important, and you did the right thing by sending it to me immediately before it got snatched.'

Vik said, 'I believe this man is still in the city—or at least in India—or else they wouldn't have attacked us. But he'll try to escape the country soon. India isn't safe for him anymore. Can you share this photo with the airport security of all international airports, starting with Kolkata?'

Inspector Sarkar frowned at being instructed on his job but replied, 'I've already thought of that. Not only airports, but I'll inform major railway stations too.'

'Excellent. I think the criminals won't escape from you. You must also know everything about Dhiren Mondal and Manmatha Sen by now.'

'I see you're learning,' Inspector Sarkar said with a complacent smile. 'We've already looked into that. What Mr Dhiren told you was correct. He worked for the World Wildlife Fund. Based on the information he provided, Gujarat police arrested two suspects. He even accompanied them during the arrests. However, it was later found that the suspects weren't poachers but locals hired for smuggling the dead lions. Naturally, they couldn't provide any information about the gang leader. We also discovered that

Mr Dhiren was involved in a couple of arrests in Myanmar six months ago. He was truly trying hard to expose this gang. He probably found this photograph during his investigation but underestimated its importance.'

'And what about Manmatha Sen?' Vik asked.

'He was harder to trace. But nothing's impossible if you have the right network,' Inspector Sarkar said with a hint of pride. 'Manmatha was a former employee of Reuters, a leading news establishment in London. He resigned two years ago and started freelancing. His ex-colleague didn't know the exact reason for his resignation. But he was dating a colleague—Evita Evans, a TV anchor nowadays. Manmatha resigned soon after they broke up.'

'What about his family?'

'He and his sister Mrinalini were born and raised in the UK. Their parents died five years ago in a car crash. His sister lives with her husband and kids in Belfast. However, she's not on good terms with Manmatha and hasn't been in touch with him for the last three years. She refused to say why.'

'Any relatives or friends in India?'

'Not that I know of.'

'When did he come to India?'

'His landlord said his flat has been locked for six months. The landlord wasn't too concerned, as the rent for the entire year had been paid in advance. Manmatha stayed alone.'

'What about the house in Loudon Street?'

'That house belongs to a Marwari businessman named Ramesh Agarwal, who lives in Dubai. His agent, Kumar, manages his properties in India. He told us that Manmatha rented the house two years ago and has occupied it since. The rent has always been paid on time.'

'Yes, his servant Ratan also said he keeps travelling,' Vik noted.

Inspector Sarkar suddenly seemed to realise he had divulged too much information. He straightened up and said, 'That's enough of a lesson for one day. We're investigating Manmatha further. I'll also speak to Behala police station about Nayan Studio. Thanks for contributing to the case, but we'll take it from here. I suggest you both head straight home and avoid running any more errands. If you're attacked again, don't expect me to rescue you. There's a taxi stand outside.'

I had had enough for one day. Right now, all I wanted was the cosy bed in my room.

***

An uneasy feeling settled over me as the taxi pulled up in front of our house. The front door was wide open, though we knew our parents were at a movie and weren't expected back for another hour.

Vik let out a sharp yelp and dashed inside. I was hot on his heels, my pulse quickening. At first glance, the house didn't seem to have been ransacked. But something was amiss. Vik ran straight to his bedroom, and I hurried after him, finding him crouched over his desk drawer, tugging at the lock.

'Thank God,' Vik muttered, exhaling in relief as the drawer was found safely locked.

That's when I noticed the glaring absence. 'Vik, where's your computer?' I asked, my voice rising. 'Are you so focused on that drawer that you haven't realised the desktop is missing?'

The desk wasn't empty. The monitor, keyboard, mouse, and speakers were still there—but the CPU was gone. My stomach churned as my gaze shifted to a white sheet of paper left on the desk. The words *STAY AWAY* were scrawled on it in what I first thought was red paint. But on closer inspection, my throat tightened—it wasn't paint. The semi-dried blood gave off a metallic odour that turned my stomach.

Vik grabbed the cordless phone and dialled Inspector Sarkar immediately. We sat grimly in the living room, the tension thick, until the inspector arrived about thirty minutes later.

'Now you understand the consequences of playing detective, I suppose?' Inspector Sarkar asked in a supercilious tone.

Vik remained silent; his jaw clenched.

The Inspector continued, 'All the same, you've stirred the hornet's nest. The same thing happened at Nayan Studio about an hour ago. Two men entered the shop at gunpoint and stole the computer CPU. Someone doesn't want this photo reaching the authorities.'

Both of us were startled.

'The gang must have more members than we anticipated,' Vik said darkly. 'Otherwise, they couldn't have launched three attacks in such a short span. They must have tailed us from Kiran's house this afternoon and saw us visit the studio. Neither we nor Mr Mondal's family are safe until this gang is apprehended.'

'How did they find out where we live?' I asked, dread creeping into my voice.

'They've likely stationed lookouts near Mr Mondal's house,' Vik replied. 'They could have followed us yesterday evening or this morning. Our house might even be under surveillance. Inspector Sarkar, we need protection.'

Inspector Sarkar nodded; his expression steely. 'Rest assured, I'll get all of them soon. Airports are already on high alert, and the photo has been circulated. I won't let them slip through the net. In the meantime, I'll station a plainclothes constable at your house and Anshu Sir's residence.'

'Thank you,' Vik said earnestly. 'Will you also keep me

updated on the case? You can reach us on the landline.'

Inspector Sarkar smirked; his tone laced with irony. 'You've got some nerve to ask for that,' he paused, then added, 'But I suppose you've earned it by recovering that photo. Just don't do anything stupid.'

***

Mom and Dad returned a while later. We didn't tell them what had happened. The thieves had picked the lock to enter, so the door wasn't damaged. Vik had already thrown away the blood-scrawled threat message. When Dad asked about the computer, Vik replied that he had sent it for repair.

Even though I knew a constable in plain clothes was stationed outside, keeping an eye on the house, I couldn't shake the feeling of unease. Vik urged me to act naturally, but I found it challenging. After dinner, I decided to retreat to my room early.

Shortly after, Vik came in and asked, 'Where's your tablet, Rik?'

'In my school bag.'

'Can you give it to me?'

'One minute.'

I understood why he needed it. With his phone and computer stolen, Vik had no access to the internet. While he could have used Mom or Dad's phones, doing so would have raised questions about his missing phone.

I handed him the tablet and said, 'I still don't understand why they stole our computer. The photo wasn't in it. We hadn't even come home since we got the photo.'

Vik sighed. 'To access my email. I knew they couldn't unlock my phone, but I didn't think they'd go this far. Our desktop wasn't password-protected, and my email password was saved in the browser. They must have connected the CPU to a monitor and accessed the PC. As expected, they've deleted the mail from Nayan Studio.'

Vik turned the tablet screen towards me to show the inbox.

I stayed silent, and he continued, 'I'm sure they searched the entire house. Luckily, they didn't check your school bag. Otherwise, we'd have lost your tablet too. I was also afraid Mom and Dad's phones would be snatched before they got home. But Inspector Sarkar's prompt action—stationing a constable here—likely prevented that. By stealing the CPU, they hoped to stall my investigation, at least for tonight. And I think that's all this guy needs. He's probably planning to escape tonight or tomorrow. If Inspector Sarkar can't stop him, and the gang leader manages to leave the country, we'll never catch him.'

'At last, you agree he's the gang leader! I told you the moment I saw that photo.' I couldn't help but feel triumphant.

'Yes, from all the evidence, it seems your hunch was correct. Now, can you do some more detective work?'

'Detective work?'

'Yes, using your tab. Check what you can find about Manmatha Sen on the internet and social media. I'll be back shortly.'

Vik left the room.

I began searching for Manmatha Sen, adding the keyword *Reuters*. The search engine brought up an article he had written three years ago about endangered species and the need to preserve them. There were links to several social media profiles, most belonging to namesakes. However, I recognised the correct profile from the picture in the Loudon Street house. He didn't seem active on social media; his last post was a year old. But something caught my eye. Under a photo of him in front of Big Ben was a comment: *"Handsome as always, XOXO"* by Evita Evans.

Recognising the name of the celebrity TV anchor, I hesitated momentarily. Then, with zero expectation of a reply, I sent her a message.

Hi. Sorry to bother, but I wanted to ask you about Manmatha Sen.

To my utter surprise, a reply came almost immediately.

Yeah. What about him?

We're investigating a case about illegal hunting in India, and his name came up.

There was a pause before her next message.

Is he all right?

We're not sure. The poacher gang has already murdered a member of the World Wildlife Fund. Any information about him might help save him.

Oh my God. Where is he now? Is he safe?

We don't know. He allegedly unmasked the whole operation but was compromised before he could inform the authorities. He's probably hiding somewhere.

Tell me, how can I help you?

For a moment, I didn't know what to ask.

I heard you both broke up two years ago. Was there a specific reason? Was he not serious about you?

Is that important?

We need to understand him better—to know what kind of person he was.

Are you suspecting him? He loved wild animals. He could never be involved in hunting them. Okay, fine… he was damn serious about me. He even changed his religion, estranging his only surviving family, his sister, to marry me. My parents, orthodox Catholics, couldn't accept him all the same. It was my fault—I listened to my parents. I know he still loves me.

When did you last meet him?

Six months ago. He said he was going to India for a project and wanted to see me before he left. I was surprised because it was the first time he'd texted me since our breakup. When I met him, I realised he hadn't looked at another girl. He was still wearing the locket I'd gifted him. Oh dear, I hope he's safe.

I didn't know what else to say.

Thanks for your help. We'll contact you if we need more information.

I'll pray for him. Please let me know once you find him.

'Finished your job, Rik?' Vik asked, walking into my room.

'Yes, but where were you?' I asked, handing him the tablet.

'I went next door to meet Mr Amit Neogi. He's a photographer and an expert in photo editing. We've become friends recently. Now, what do we have here?'

His expression grew grim as he scanned the messages.

Returning the tablet, he said darkly, 'I suspected this long ago. Ask her to send a picture of the locket she gave him, if possible.'

'What will you do with it?'

'Just do as I say. I'll explain later.'

'So, you suspected something? Do you think Manmatha was compromised?'

'Mortally compromised... in other words, murdered. Manmatha Sen is dead,' Vik said before leaving the room.

***

Even though a flood of thoughts rushed through my mind as soon as I closed my eyes, the day had been long enough to wear me out. I didn't realise when I drifted off to sleep. After a short while, or so it seemed, I was awakened by Vik whispering, 'Get up, Rik. We have to go to the airport.'

'A… airport! What time is it?' I asked thickly.

'It's 6 am The gang leader is escaping to Dubai on a flight scheduled to depart at 8:50 am He's already at the airport. The security recognised him from the circulated photo. Inspector Sarkar informed me just now. His name is Maximo Lombardi, according to his passport. His nationality is Italian.'

'But… what will Mom say? She must have heard the landline ringing. She'll never…'

'Ssshh… listen carefully. I slept with the cordless phone next to me. She didn't hear it ring. Get ready in five minutes and tell Mom you're going to the playground. I'll be waiting outside for you. Give me your tab.'

I was about to ask what he'd tell Mom, but I noticed he was already dressed in gym attire. He slipped my tablet into his backpack and hurried out.

Ten minutes later, we were speeding towards the airport in a cab. Vik remained silent throughout the journey, lost in thought. I didn't dare interrupt.

The international terminal was bustling, with a long queue of passengers waiting to enter.

'Have you told Inspector Sarkar we're coming?' I asked as we stepped out of the cab.

'No. Do you think he'd allow us?'

'What are we going to do, then? We can't even go inside without tickets.'

'I haven't figured that out yet. Let's wait here. After Inspector Sarkar arrests Maximo, they'll come out through this gate. Want some ice cream?'

Before I could respond, Vik walked airily to an ice cream kiosk and bought two cones. As he handed one to me, I asked, 'Can't you call Inspector Sarkar to check if Maximo has been arrested?'

'Patience, Rik. It's barely been five minutes since we got here. And don't forget—my phone was snatched yesterday,' Vik said testily.

I sighed, resigning myself to the wait. Vik opened my tablet and muttered, 'Evita hasn't replied yet about the locket picture,' He became engrossed in the screen while I watched the passengers trudging towards the entrance. Time dragged on, or so it felt, as we stood there without sign of Inspector Sarkar or Maximo.

Then, at long last, a commotion erupted inside the terminal. Through the glass façade, I spotted a man bolting towards the entrance with three men chasing him. One of them was shouting, 'Stop him! Stop him!'

'Hold this,' Vik said, thrusting the tab into my hands before striding forward.

The officer checking the passports at the entrance looked baffled at this unprecedented chaos and the soldier with a submachine gun beside him seemed equally perplexed. The escaping man took advantage of the situation and rushed through the entry gate, jostling the officer, the soldier and the passengers in the front of the queue. Chaos broke out instantly. Many of them lost their balance and bumped into each other. An older woman was on all fours.

Then I saw his face—the same face from the photograph. It was Maximo. Behind him, Inspector Sarkar was caught in the melee, struggling to catch up.

Where was Vik?

Suddenly, a leg shot out from the throng, sweeping Maximo off his feet. He stumbled and crashed headlong to the ground. Before he could recover, Inspector Sarkar and his men had pounced on him.

It was Vik's leg that had tripped him. Inspector Sarkar's

puzzled expression was fleeting before he said, 'Well done, Mr Chatterjee. So, you came.'

'Yes, I had to,' Vik replied.

Maximo growled, 'You have no right to do this. I have diplomatic immunity.'

The officers' grips slackened, and Inspector Sarkar hesitated, his brow furrowed.

Maximo shook free and barked, 'This is how you treat diplomats? I'll inform my embassy!'

Vik, calm as ever, said, 'You're not a diplomat. You're not even a foreigner.'

Maximo, oblivious to Vik's presence so far, looked at him and was startled momentarily as if he was seeing a ghost. The next moment he hissed, his face incensed, 'What do you mean? Who the hell are you?'

'You know me very well and also what I meant.' Vik replied as if amused.

Inspector Sarkar, visibly irked, interjected, 'What are you talking about? Based on your suggestion, we arrested this gentleman. If he's a diplomat, we'll be in serious trouble.'

'You won't be,' Vik assured him. 'Let me explain. Can we move somewhere quieter? The police van will do.'

Still unsure, Inspector Sarkar instructed his men to escort Maximo to the van parked across the road. We followed them, attracting curious glances from onlookers.

Inside the van, Maximo's seething rage was palpable as he muttered curses under his breath. Vik calmly reached into his backpack, pulling out a bottle labelled 'Doctor's Spirit' and a small white cloth.

'Prosthetic makeup takes time to remove completely, but this should suffice,' Vik said. 'Hold his hands.'

Despite Maximo's resistance and foul-mouthed protests, Vik soaked the cloth and vigorously rubbed it against his face. The van filled with the chemical smell of the spirit. The cloth darkened, and a thin layer of synthetic skin soon began peeling away.

'Would you kindly remove your wig and contact lenses, or should I?' Vik asked.

There was no need. A familiar face emerged as the layers came off, leaving Inspector Sarkar and me stunned.

'You chose the wrong career,' Vik said coldly. 'You could have been a great actor given the finesse with which you staged your murder.'

Still sporting his green contact lenses and curly grey wig, Dhiren Uncle looked like an injured leopard.

***

I spent the day with curiosity simmering within me. We returned home soon after the arrest because Vik insisted, he couldn't skip college today. Inspector Sarkar wanted him to come to the police station to explain things. Still, Vik said he would provide a summarised explanation over the phone from college and save the detailed clarification for the afternoon. I also had to attend school, which meant no answers to the flood of questions racing through my mind. By the time I got home, after an utterly fruitless day of inattentive lessons and scolding from teachers, my mind felt like it would explode.

At 5 pm, we gathered in Mr Mondal's room. Mr Mondal, Rajen Uncle, Krishna Aunty, Kiran, Mr Shamick, Inspector Sarkar, Dad, Vik, and I were present. The air was grimmer than ever. All the family members looked miserable, particularly Mr Mondal.

He began sombrely, 'I am disgraced by my son's treachery. I

would have preferred him dead. None of us will enjoy discussing this, but we must know the truth. Asit has done a wonderful job, but he would agree that my son could not have been brought to justice without Victor's intervention. Victor, we all want to hear from you.'

Vik straightened in his chair, 'I'll explain everything, but before that, I'd like an update on what's happened since the arrest, from Inspector Sarkar.'

Inspector Sarkar said, 'We haven't taken a detailed statement from Mr Dhiren yet as he claimed to feel unwell. However, he's already given us the names of his accomplices. Six were hiding in Kolkata to do his bidding. We raided a cheap hotel in Sealdah and arrested them all. A few more are based in Gujarat; their details have been shared with the Gujarat police. Your phone, CPU, and the Nayan Studio CPU were recovered from the same hotel. You'll have your belongings back by tonight. Also, we arrested Ratan from the Loudon Street house. His real name is Abani, and he was Mr Dhiren's right-hand man.'

I sat up straighter. So, we truly had entered the enemy's den!

'Did you get the photo from the Rajasthan police I asked for?' Vik inquired.

'Yes, here it is.' Sarkar took out his phone.

Vik turned to me, 'Did Evita send you a reply?'

'Yes. I saw it after I returned from school,' I replied.

At Vik's instruction, I handed him my tablet. He held the tab and Inspector Sarkar's phone side by side, showing the room the two photos. Both depicted the same metallic crucifix locket, albeit at different angles.

He began, 'A man was shot, his body burnt and dumped in a village near the Rajasthan border around the same time the lions were smuggled. At first, it seemed coincidental, but I took an interest. Now, as you can see, the locket that Manmatha's ex-girlfriend gifted him, and the one recovered from the burnt body are strikingly similar. Of course, the final proof will require a DNA match between the corpse and Manmatha's sister. But you can break the bad news to Evita.'

Seeing my grimace, Vik added gently, 'I know it's difficult, Rik, but she deserves to know.'

He scanned the room, taking a deep breath. 'Let me lay it all out, partly from evidence and deduction. I've already given Inspector Sarkar a brief overview, but I'll repeat the entire story for everyone. As we know, Mr Dhiren Mondal was the leader of the poacher gang that had operated in this region for years. His position in the World Wildlife Fund provided him access to critical information and resources, which he used to orchestrate his illegal activities. That's why this gang was so elusive. Whenever the police compromised their operations, he pretended to help them by giving up minor accomplices—locals hired for smuggling—while shielding the core gang. This tactic worked in both Myanmar and Gujarat. However, the real problem arose when a young journalist and wildlife enthusiast came to India and, perhaps, uncovered the entire operation. I'm unsure how much Manmatha had discovered or whether he shared any information with the authorities. Regardless, his existence posed a threat to the gang. I don't know who pulled the trigger, but Dhiren Uncle consented to it, making him no less than a murderer.'

Mr Mondal sighed heavily. Kiran and his parents looked stricken. Mr Shamick frowned, shaking his head.

Vik continued, 'Manmatha's body was burned beyond recognition and dumped in a deserted field near Bhalgaon. They failed to notice the locket he was wearing—a crucial oversight. But I'll come back to that. I suspect Manmatha may have managed to pass some information to the authorities before his death, information that could eventually have compromised the entire gang. That's why simply eliminating him wasn't enough for Dhiren Uncle. He had to flee the country and reinvent himself with a new identity. Keeping his original identity was out of the question, as both the World Wildlife Fund and Interpol could trace him anywhere. So, Dhiren Mondal had to 'die' in the eyes of the world.

'After returning to Kolkata, he began spreading terror at home, using what was likely animal blood to make it appear as though someone was trying to intimidate the family. He also needed a scapegoat for his fake murder, and he chose poor Manmatha for the role. Dhiren Uncle probably gathered enough information about him through torture or by examining his phone, belongings, and documents. The house on Loudon Street was staged to look like Manmatha's residence. I don't believe Manmatha had ever set foot in Kolkata, let alone rented a house here.'

Inspector Sarkar interjected, 'The house belongs to Ramesh Agarwal, a businessman based in Dubai. He's the elder brother of one of the gang members. Ramesh was persuaded to tell the police that he had rented the house to Manmatha Sen. Naturally, he's beyond our reach, even after providing a false statement.'

Vik picked up the thread, 'The house was sparsely decorated with locally purchased items to create the illusion of a bachelor journalist's residence. A single photo of Manmatha was taken from social media, printed, and framed to place in the living room. Dhiren Uncle likely intended to mislead the police with fabricated information, so that after his staged death, they'd end up chasing a wild goose. When Mr Mondal called me instead of the police, it didn't disrupt his plan. He fed me that made-up story, gave me Manmatha's fake address, and asked me to inform the police if anything happened to him. I believed him and took the bait. He even left a fake letter on his desk, ensuring it would be discovered easily. Then… well, I think you all have a fair idea of how he staged his murder.'

I said, 'Not at all. I have several doubts. A knife was seen stabbed into his heart to its hilt. How could that possibly be staged?'

Vik chuckled, 'Let me show you something. I picked this up from a shop on my way back from college today.'

He produced what appeared to be the hilt of a knife. To my astonishment, there was no blade attached. Instead, a plastic sucker—like those used in hooks or car mobile holders—was affixed to it.

'It's a straightforward trick,' Vik explained. 'These are commonly used as props in theatre. Tear your shirt a little, press the sucker onto your chest, and apply a bit of red ink to your shirt. Voilà—you got yourself murdered.' With an amused glint, he added, 'Of course, Dhiren Uncle didn't use red ink.'

Inspector Sarkar interrupted, his voice tinged with confusion, 'But the blood collected from the crime scene was undoubtedly his. Even the DNA test confirms it's a match. How is that possible?'

Vik replied, 'I think all the family members here would agree he looked unusually pale after returning from his trip. Wouldn't you?'

Everyone nodded in agreement.

Rajen Uncle exclaimed, 'I even examined him. He was significantly anaemic. I urged him to get a blood test immediately, but he assured me he would do it soon.'

'Well, there's your answer,' Vik said. 'Dhiren Uncle had collected and preserved his blood beforehand, much like in a blood donation drive. That blood was used to stage the murder.

However, he likely drew more than a typical donation, which explains why he appeared so pale.'

'My God,' Dad exclaimed, his eyes wide with shock.

Vik continued, 'He didn't play dead because his doctor brother would have easily uncovered the truth. He knew that when Rajen Uncle saw him panting for his last breaths, he would instinctively rush to call an ambulance without examining him closely. His henchmen were hiding behind the trees nearby. One of them subdued Krishna Aunty with a carotid hold, rendering her unconscious. Then, as planned, they carried Dhiren Uncle away. The entire act was orchestrated so meticulously that it almost looked real.'

'Almost?' I demanded.

'Yes. I'll point out the flaw in the plan shortly. Now, where were we? Ah, yes. After that night's charade, Ratan, or rather Abani, Dhiren Uncle's right-hand man, carried out the next part of the act. Posing as a caretaker in Manmatha's fabricated house, he subtly shifted suspicion onto the poor, deceased journalist. The plan proceeded smoothly and would have succeeded if not for the sharp eyes of my younger brother, Ritwik, who spotted the Nayan Studio envelope.' Vik patted me on the back.

I felt a surge of instant jubilation.

Vik said, 'The photograph was taken when Dhiren Uncle created a fake passport under the alias Maximo Lombardi. He chose a little-known studio for the photo, likely to avoid drawing attention. He used prosthetic makeup, which can completely alter a person's appearance. I believe one of the gang members is a makeup artist since applying prosthetics requires considerable expertise. There are many ways to obtain a fake passport. Inspector Sarkar can better explain where and how it's done in this city.'

Sarkar nodded.

After a brief pause, Vik continued, 'The discovery of Maximo Lombardi's photograph caused the gang to panic—which often leads to mistakes. Their anxiety was understandable since Dhiren Uncle was scheduled to pass through airport security the next morning as Maximo. I don't know whether Abani or Dhiren Uncle himself ordered the attack on us and the subsequent burglaries, but it was a misstep. It heightened our awareness of the photo's importance, prompting Inspector Sarkar to circulate it among airport security and initiate surveillance. Dhiren Uncle likely believed he had bought time by preventing me from handing the photo to the authorities. He didn't anticipate how quickly the photo would be shared at the airport. Desperation drove him to make his escape attempt, but thanks to Inspector Sarkar's swift action and his efficient team, it didn't succeed.'

Inspector Sarkar returned a wan smile, knowing Vik was only trying to be modest.

Finally, breaking his silence, Mr Mondal asked, 'But how did you piece everything together, Victor? What clues led you to suspect Dhiren?'

Vik smiled and said, 'I was waiting for that question. Dhiren Uncle's plan was ingenious, no doubt. There were only a handful of clues, and I agree that discovering the photograph was pivotal in solving the case. But it wasn't the only clue. Throughout the investigation, I encountered several seemingly insignificant details. Individually, they might have appeared trivial, but when pieced together, they painted a much larger picture.

'The most glaring clue was right in front of us from the very beginning: the excessive amount of blood at the murder scene. To understand why that's unusual, you need to know that a knife can cause two types of injuries—stabs or slices. Slicing wounds, also known as incised wounds, are superficial and cause external bleeding, often creating a gruesome crime scene with significant blood, as we see in cases of throat slashing. On the other hand, stab wounds typically cause internal bleeding into the body cavities, such as the chest or abdomen, with minimal external blood loss. Therefore, the crime scene wouldn't usually be so messy.

'None of the gang members, including Dhiren Uncle, seemed aware of this basic forensic principle, leading them to overdo the staging with an excessive amount of blood. Although I noticed this anomaly early on, it didn't immediately occur to me—though it should have—that the entire scene was staged.

'I started suspecting foul play when I examined the letter. I realised it had been dictated. This indicated that the person dictating the message didn't want their handwriting to be recognised. Interestingly, the person dictating the message paused four times, saying just two lines. Coincidentally—or perhaps not—Dhiren Uncle had a similar habit of pausing frequently when speaking.

'Then, I found the cash memos. They detailed the purchase of 45 books on media and mass communication—topics typically associated with journalism—dated the same day as Dhiren Uncle's return from his tour. When I visited Manmatha's fake house on Loudon Street, I noticed there were precisely 45 books on journalism on the bookshelf. That was far too much of a coincidence. It was then I first realised Manmatha might already be dead.

'The final clue was a dead giveaway. The gang had overdone the setup at Manmatha's fake house, just as they had with the crime scene. The prayer area in the living room was a key inconsistency. It's likely the Marwari house owner had built the prayer space, and the gang foolishly placed idols of Hindu gods there to make it appear lived-in. When I asked Abani who worshipped the idols, he said it was Manmatha. That was a blatant mistake—Manmatha had converted to Christianity three years ago. The gang hadn't noticed the crucifix locket he always wore, even when they killed him.

'When I read the chat between Rik and Evita, the entire picture came into focus. I even sought help from a friend who's a Photoshop expert. I had him compare the photographs of Maximo and Dhiren Uncle, half-expecting some similarities. Unfortunately, he explained that prosthetic makeup has advanced to the point where it can completely alter someone's appearance, making it impossible to prove they're the same person through Photoshop alone.

'At that point, I realised it was up to Inspector Sarkar to bring Dhiren Uncle to justice, and I was confident he wouldn't let him escape. That's all I have to say.'

Inspector Sarkar finally looked smug. Vik certainly knew how to strike the right chord.

I asked, 'Where did you get Maximo's picture? Your phone was stolen, and the email was deleted.'

'That was easy. My phone gallery automatically backs up to the cloud so that I can access the photos from any device.'

'And where did you get Dhiren Uncle's picture?'

For a fleeting moment, Vik gave me a look that clearly said, *Really?* Then, turning to Mr Mondal with a sheepish smile, he confessed, 'I must admit to something… less than ethical. While you were quizzing me about my detective skills, I secretly clicked pictures of everyone in the house. I promise I'll delete them once I have my phone back.'

That's why he'd been subtly occupied with his phone during the so-called test.

Mr Mondal didn't seem upset, though Dad gave a disapproving nod. I felt a twinge of embarrassment for even asking.

For the first time, Inspector Sarkar sounded genuinely admiring as he said, ‘I must admit, Victor, you’re a remarkable detective. Consider getting a license.’

He then turned to Mr Mondal and added, ‘Sir, I must take my leave. There’s plenty to do before your son is presented in court tomorrow.’

Mr Mondal nodded silently.

***

After Inspector Sarkar left, Mr Anshu said, ‘I must thank you, Victor. Appointing you for this case was the best decision I could have made. I wish you all the best for your future.’

Dad was about to stand up, but Vik stopped him, ‘Wait, Dad. I’m not done yet. Only half of the case has been discussed. Has everyone forgotten about the blue sapphire?’

Everyone froze in place. Truth be told, I had forgotten entirely about the sapphire amidst the turmoil.

‘Have you found it?’ Rajen Uncle asked, his voice brimming with expectation.

‘Yes.’

Now, the room was charged with silent excitement.

I stared at Vik, utterly astonished. When did he find the sapphire?

‘Where is it?’ Krishna Aunty asked, her voice barely above a whisper.

Vik paused, then said, ‘Before I reveal that, let me return something that belongs to Mr Shamick.’

Mr Shamick, who had been quiet until now, looked up, startled.

Vik pulled a snuff-box from his pocket and handed it to him.

'This is yours. There's no point denying it. Even your initials are engraved on it.'

Mr Shamick took the snuffbox, opened it, and looked inside. The fleeting spark of excitement in his eyes was quickly replaced by despair—and a trace of anger.

Vik smirked, 'What you're looking for isn't there anymore.'

'What's going on? I'm not following any of this!' Mr Mondal exclaimed, his face a mask of confusion.

Vik cleared his throat, 'Let me explain. The day Mr Shamick went to check on the sapphire, it was still in the box. He took it himself and placed it in his snuffbox, tossing the snuff out of the window. Then, he returned here, screaming that the sapphire had been stolen.'

'Liar!' Mr Shamick shot up; his face flushed with rage, 'Where's your proof?' he demanded.

'I'm the proof,' Vik replied calmly. 'I noticed traces of snuff powder on the windowsill. I also observed that after the incident, you stopped snuffing, even though you'd been using it every few minutes before. That made me sure you had hidden the sapphire in your snuffbox.

'While we were going downstairs, you were walking right behind me. I pretended to trip, and as you caught me to steady my fall, I pickpocketed the snuffbox. I didn't reveal it at the time because Mr Mondal was already devastated, believing his son was dead. I decided it was best to keep it safe for the time being.'

Disappointment was written all over Mr Mondal's face. He said coldly, 'I didn't expect this from you, Shamick.'

Mr Shamick slumped back into his chair, burying his face in his hands. Between sobs, he said, 'Forgive me, Anshu. Greed got the better of me. I've regretted it ever since.'

I suddenly realised something and blurted out, 'That's why

you focused on your desk drawer after the burglary. You weren't worried about the desktop—you were checking if the sapphire was still there!'

'Right you are, Rik,' Vik said, nodding.

He reached into his pocket and pulled out something wrapped in tissue paper. Carefully, he unwrapped it, revealing the brilliant blue sapphire. The gem sparkled in the light, casting shimmering hues of red and blue around the room, momentarily transforming its aura.

A Deadly Quest for Justice

Avay received a dispatch call while we were having evening tea. He was Vik's friend, a newly appointed cop in the homicide department. His face tightened as he disconnected the call, a shadow of nervousness flickering across it.

'Any problem, bro?' Vik asked casually but with a hint of curiosity.

'Yeah,' Avay replied, rubbing the back of his neck. 'I just got my first murder case. I'm a bit nervous—can't afford to mess it up.'

He hesitated momentarily, glancing at Vik with hope and reluctance, 'Hey, I know it's a lot to ask, but… could you come with me? You've dealt with this kind of thing before.'

Vik smirked, leaning back in his chair. 'Ordinary homicides aren't my thing. But for you, I'll make an exception. On one condition—Rik comes with us.'

A thrill shot through me. This evening was about to get interesting.

Avay looked torn for a second, then gave a slight nod. 'Alright, fair enough.'

Vik turned to me, his tone brisk. 'Three minutes, Rik. Get ready.'

Heart racing, I bolted to my room to change.

***

Half an hour later, we alighted from the police jeep in New Town, where the incident had occurred.

Avay, being the first officer on the scene, led the way. The crime scene was a garden house tucked away at the end of a quiet, less-travelled lane.

A crowd had gathered in front of the house, murmuring in hushed tones. A lone constable struggled to hold them back, his voice hoarse from repeating the exact instructions. We crossed the police line, drawing curious glances from the onlookers. Vik and I faced a few raised eyebrows, but Avay waved the constable off, explaining that we were with him.

The garden was sprawling, its paths shaded by thick, old trees. The curved porch obscured the entrance from view, lending the place an unsettling air. Poor lighting made it difficult to take in the details.

Two constables stood guard at the front door, which was slightly ajar.

'What happened here? Tell me in brief,' Avay asked.

One of the constables stepped forward, his voice low but steady, 'Sir, the victim is Harinath Sen, an elderly widower who lived here with his only son. He was found in his bedroom with his throat slit. It's… a horrific scene. Blood is everywhere. His son, Ranadip, discovered the body when he returned from work.'

'I see. Has anyone witnessed anything unusual?'

'Not seen, sir. But heard.'

'Explain.'

'Earlier this evening, a notorious local goon came here alone. The house backs onto a park on the west side, where people often walk. Several people heard shouting coming from inside, including… uh… threats to kill. A few even saw the man ride away on a bike shortly after the shouting stopped. But no one dared enter the house.'

'Who is this goon? I need a name.'

The constable hesitated but continued, 'It took some coaxing, sir. The locals were too scared to speak at first. A shopkeeper at the corner finally gave us a name, and others confirmed it afterwards. They're still terrified, though. I'm not sure they'll testify. The man is Nahar Malik.'

'Damn,' Avay muttered, 'He's a tough one to get. The ruling party shields him.'

'Not this time, sir,' the constable said with defiance, puffing out his chest. 'We found the murder weapon on site. If we can lift fingerprints—'

'Excellent. Where's the forensic team?'

'On their way, sir.'

'Good. Does anyone else live here?'

'No, sir. The son is unmarried, and the servants don't live in. They leave by midday.'

Avay nodded, signalling for us to proceed. We passed the constables and stepped into the house.

The living room was unexpectedly pristine—spacious, tastefully decorated, and spotless. It felt worlds away from the horror described outside, a sharp contrast that was almost unnerving. The family was well-off.

Vik leaned toward me and whispered, 'Don't touch anything, Rik. This is a crime scene.'

I rolled my eyes. Even as a high schooler, I knew better than to tamper with evidence.

'Nahar Malik,' Avay began grimly, 'is one of the most notorious criminals in Kolkata. Name any crime, and he's done it—murder, rape, assault, threats—you name it. There are multiple charges against him but no convictions. He's been arrested five times and walked free each time due to lack of evidence. Witnesses always turn hostile at the last minute, usually after receiving threats. We can't get him without solid proof. This murder weapon might be our only hope.'

Vik nodded. 'Yes, I've heard of him too. Let's see what we can find here. Rik, you can wait in the living room if you don't want to see the body.'

'No way,' I snapped. 'I'm coming with you. I don't shudder at the sight of blood.'

***

A chill ran down my spine as we stepped into the main bedroom. The sight was nothing short of grotesque. Blood spattered the walls like a macabre piece of modern art, framing Harinath's lifeless body on the bed. His throat was slashed clean through, with semi-dried blood forming a crimson collar around his neck. The bed beneath him was drenched in a dark pool of blood, and the wall near his head bore splatters that might have been perfect for a horror movie poster.

'I think both carotid arteries were severed,' Vik remarked, staring intently at the gruesome pattern on the wall.

'Yeah, that seems likely,' agreed the forensic examiner, who had already begun his work. He crouched by the body, inspecting it with a practised eye. 'A single, precise cut—deep and deliberate. The killer had a steady hand. Judging by the angle, I'd say the victim was lying down when it happened. Maybe the assailant forced him onto the bed before making the fatal cut.'

'Any other injuries?' Avay asked, his tone professional but edged with curiosity.

The examiner's gloved hands moved over the body, 'Hmm... wait. Yes, there are multiple rib fractures. Blunt force trauma.

Likely caused by one or more powerful punches to the chest.'

'A forceful punch—or several,' Vik mused, his brow furrowed. 'Enough to knock him onto the bed, perhaps?'

'Quite possible,' the examiner replied.

Avay glanced around the room. 'Where's the murder weapon?'

A constable standing just behind us spoke up. 'Here it is, sir. On the table over there.' He pointed toward a sofa set in the corner of the room.

The setup was oddly domestic. The oval glass-topped table bore a fruit platter laden with oranges and apples, and beside it lay a large kitchen knife, its blade glinting dully under the light, soaked in dried blood. One of the apples had been sliced in half but left uneaten.

'Looks like he was interrupted while preparing to eat,' Avay observed grimly. 'The apple's cut, but he didn't get a chance to take a bite. And then, the same knife...' He trailed off.

'...was used to end his life,' Vik finished, his tone flat but weighted. 'It suggests the killer didn't come here planning murder. Maybe it started as a threat, but things escalated. The knife was just... conveniently there.'

The forensic examiner carefully picked up the knife with gloved hands and slipped it into a plastic evidence bag. He swabbed the tabletop for blood before continuing his examination.

Meanwhile, Vik began systematically inspecting the room, his sharp eyes missing nothing. The rest of the space was eerily tidy. Harinath, an older man, hadn't stood a chance against his assailant. The broken ribs, the signs of struggle on the bed—everything pointed to a quick, brutal attack. To me, it seemed straightforward. A seasoned goon like Nahar Malik wouldn't have had much trouble overpowering someone like Harinath. The knife, if it bore Nahar's fingerprints, could be enough to convict him despite his notorious connections. Avay, visibly more confident now, squared his shoulders, likely feeling he'd cracked his first homicide case. The only real challenge would be ensuring the evidence held up against the pressure of Nahar's powerful allies.

Vik, however, seemed less inclined to settle for the obvious. Slipping on gloves borrowed from the forensic team, he combed through the room with methodical precision. He opened the attached bathroom door and peeked inside. I followed, curious about what he was looking for.

The bathroom was damp, with a pool of water still visible in the bathing area. A wet towel hung limply from a rack. It seemed Harinath had taken a bath not long before the attack.

The bed told a story of its own—messy sheets and rumpled pillows hinted at a violent struggle. As Vik scanned the floor near the bathroom door, he suddenly crouched, his gaze fixed on something small. I followed his line of sight and spotted it, too: a single drop of dried blood on the floor. The forensic examiner hurried over to collect a sample.

'Let's check the rest of the house,' Vik said briskly.

The house was modest but well-kept. It was a two-story building. The ground floor had a spacious living room with an open kitchen, the bedroom where the murder had occurred, and a shared guest bathroom. Upstairs were two bedrooms—one used by Harinath's son, Ranadip and the other serving as a guest room—each with attached bathrooms.

In the open kitchen, Vik stopped by the minibar. Six glasses were arranged neatly on the counter. One by one, he picked them up and sniffed. He also smelled the kitchen sink. His expression darkened slightly, his frown deepening.

Curious, I picked up one of the glasses and followed his lead.

A strange odour lingered in two of them, faint but unmistakable. I was also about to smell the sink, but Vik's sharp glance stopped me.

'Can we talk to the son and the witnesses?' Vik asked Avay, breaking the silence.

Avay nodded, 'That's next on my list. Let's go.'

***

We settled in the living room as Avay called for Harinath's son first. Ranadip walked in, visibly shaken. His tall, lean frame seemed to carry the weight of grief, and his rimless spectacles magnified his dark, tired eyes.

He was in his thirties, dressed in formal attire, with his clean-shaven face betraying the strain of the evening.

Avay began, calm but direct, 'Did you return home from your workplace today?'

'Yes, of course,' Ranadip replied, his voice wavering.

'Tell me what you saw when you arrived.'

'The door wasn't locked, and...' His voice faltered as he covered his face with his hand, 'Dad... it was horrific.' He drew a trembling breath, 'Please, officer, make sure that monster hangs for this.'

'Don't worry. We'll do our job. But tell me—do you know why anyone would threaten or kill your father?'

Ranadip hesitated, then spoke, his voice breaking. 'It's because of me. It's all my fault.'

'Your fault? How?' Vik interjected, leaning forward slightly.

'The local political leader, Badal Gupta, sent this goon. I'm actively involved with the opposition party. I protested against his illegal activities, and this... this is his way of silencing me, showing his power. But why my father? Why kill him?' He shook his head, his anguish turning to frustration. 'This man, Nahar, is a monster. Everyone knows that. He takes pleasure in killing people. No one is safe with him roaming free.'

Vik asked, 'Your family seems well-off. Are you in business?'

'No, I work in the corporate sector. Our wealth comes from Dad's investments in the share market. That was his focus all day.'

'Did he have close friends?'

'Yes, a few college friends used to visit. Siddharth Uncle was the most frequent—he lives nearby.'

'Did he come today?'

'I don't know. But I saw him outside a while ago. He probably heard about the incident and came. The police aren't letting anyone inside. I was waiting outside, too.'

'Alright. You can step out and wait again. Ask this Siddharth Uncle to come in for questioning,' Avay instructed.

An older man, maybe in his sixties, entered next. He was tall and stout, with grey hair and a thick grey moustache. He sneezed as he entered and sneezed several times during the interrogation as if he had caught a cold. He occasionally rubbed at faint red marks on his face and hands, the only visible parts of his skin. He probably had an allergy. He was well dressed, wearing a blazer, trousers, and boots. He was holding a briefcase.

He introduced himself as Dr. Siddharth Rana, a retired army doctor. He had served in the Indian Army for many years and retired as a major. Now, he had a limited private practice. He was a childhood friend of Harinath, and after he moved to New Town, he became their family physician. He lived alone. His only family was his son, who lived in New York with his wife and kids.

After the introduction, Vik asked, 'Did you visit him often?'

'At least three times a week. I came here today to see him...

but now...' His voice cracked, and tears welled up in his eyes.

'You were his doctor. How was his health?'

'Not good. He had a heart attack a few months ago and was on several medications. Honestly, I didn't think he'd survive another attack. But this... this horrific death... God!' He shook his head, grief etched on his face.

'He was wealthy. Who inherits his estate?'

'His son, Ranadip. Hari made a will to ensure it, and I signed as a witness.'

'How was their relationship?'

'Generally fine. But they argued occasionally about Ranadip's political involvement. Hari wasn't happy about it.'

'What do you know about Nahar Malik?'

Dr Rana straightened slightly. 'Look, I'm a doctor. My only interest is in my patients, not politics. But I've heard of him—a dangerous criminal, or so they say. That's all I know.'

Avay's gaze shifted to the briefcase. 'Were you heading to see another patient after this?'

'No, it's for Hari. He called me this morning, saying he wasn't feeling well. So, I came to check on him.'

'Where were you earlier this evening, between five and six?'

'I was at home.'

'Alright. You can go now.'

Avay glanced at his notes before calling the next witness. 'Rajen, step in.'

The grocery shop owner from across the street shuffled into the room, his wiry frame and tired face reflecting years of hard work. Thin and elderly, with curly grey hair that framed his weary expression, he wore a plain white shirt and black trousers, a modest yet neat appearance.

'Tell us what you saw and heard,' Avay prompted.

'Around 5:15 pm, I saw Nahar Malik arrive on a bike. He parked at the front gate and went inside. After a few minutes, I heard loud voices—shouting. He left around 5:25 pm.' Rajen fidgeted with the hem of his shirt as he spoke, his voice thin but steady.

'Did you catch what was being said?'

'No, sir. My shop is too far. People in the park might have heard something.'

'What time did Harinath's son arrive?'

'About an hour later, sir.'

'And after that?'

'He came out screaming, maybe ten minutes later. I stepped out of my shop, and a crowd gathered within minutes. Neighbours and passersby entered the garden. The police arrived half an hour later.'

'Did anyone else enter the house before Ranadip?'

'I don't think so, sir. My shop faces the gate, and I never left my seat during that time.'

Vik asked, 'Do you keep your shop open all day?'

'No, sir. Only from 8 am to 1 pm, and 5 pm to 10 pm. I close it during lunchtime.'

Three more witnesses followed—a jogger and a young couple who had been in the park then. They all corroborated hearing shouting from the house, including threats of murder. However, most of the onlookers were reluctant to testify.

When the final witness left, a constable whispered something to Avay. His face lit up.

'We've got Nahar,' he announced. 'The cops arrested him at a nearby bar.'

'That's great,' Vik said. 'But be careful. If he has powerful backers, they'll try to sabotage the evidence and intimidate witnesses.'

'Not on my watch,' Avay replied confidently. 'Thanks for the advice anyway.'

Vik stood. 'I'll take my leave now. Keep me updated.'

'Shall I drop you home?' Avay offered.

'No, we're fine.'

We stepped outside, the air heavy with murmurs from the gathered crowd. The police were loading Harinath's body into a van as we hailed a cab.

***

Vik told the cab driver to stop five blocks from our home. I was confused as he gestured for me to get out.

'Take this alley, Rik. Come fast,' he said, his voice low but firm.

I frowned. 'What's going on?' I asked while following him.

'A car is tailing us. There might be four or five people inside. Does your smartphone take good videos?'

'Yes, but—'

'Listen carefully,' he interrupted. 'See this building under construction? Go to the first floor and position yourself near the side facing the streetlight. Stay hidden in the dark. I'll head towards the streetlight. Those people are likely here to attack me. I'll keep the action near the light so you can record their faces. Got it?'

'But, Vik, can you handle them alone? Shouldn't we—'

'Not another word. Go now before they spot you. Move!'

I didn't argue. Darting up the stairs, I reached the first floor in seconds, the unfinished building closing in around me with its heavy air and shadowed corners. My breaths quickened, part exertion, part the knot of anxiety tightening in my chest.

Vik strolled towards the streetlamp, his movements

unnervingly calm, quiet defiance in every step. I tightened my grip on the phone, forcing my trembling hands to steady. A part of me itched to call out, to warn him—but something in his unwavering stance stopped me. Fear mingled with a flicker of admiration. Who was this man who could face danger with such unshaken composure?

The shadows shifted. Four figures emerged from the alley, and their movements were calculated. One held a knife, its glint catching the faint light. Another gripped a hockey stick, swinging it lazily as if testing its weight. The third kept his hand buried in his pocket, the outline of a concealed weapon unmistakable. The fourth was a hulking brute, his bulk exuding raw intimidation.

They hesitated briefly, scanning their surroundings. For a tense moment, I thought they might spot me. Then their eyes locked on Vik, standing under the streetlight like a lone sentinel. Seeing he was alone, they advanced, their strides bold and assured, like predators closing in on prey.

One of them, the man with his hand in his pocket, drew a pistol and pointed it at Vik's chest. 'You don't know who you're messing with,' he snarled. 'Don't ever poke your nose—'

He didn't finish. Vik moved like lightning, grabbing the gun with his left hand while stepping out of the line of fire. His right hand delivered a crushing punch to the man's face, leaving him stunned. Before the assailant could react, Vik used both hands to disarm him, snapping the gun away with precision. A brutal sidekick to the chest sent the man flying several feet, landing in a heap on the ground.

The other three froze, stunned by the sudden display of skill. Vik now held the pistol, but instead of using it, he calmly ejected the magazine and tossed both pieces aside in opposite directions. It was a deliberate move, one that seemed to taunt them. Using the pistol would have complicated things, legally and otherwise—something Vik wanted to avoid.

Their hesitation evaporated, and they charged him together. Vik shifted his stance, moving in a small circle to avoid being surrounded. The man with the knife lunged first, aiming for Vik's stomach. Vik deflected the strike with his left hand and countered with a powerful punch to the attacker's jaw. In one swift motion, he locked the man's wrist in a cavalier wristlock, wrenching the knife away before driving a knee into his groin.

The muscular brute was next, closing the gap with alarming speed. He swung a heavy fist aimed at Vik's head, but Vik ducked just in time and retaliated with a slashing motion using the knife. A deep gash bloomed on the man's forearm, and he stumbled back, clutching the wound.

The man with the hockey stick hesitated, clearly unsure whether to attack. But as Vik discarded the knife, the man gained a shred of confidence and swung the stick in a wide arc. Vik dodged the first swing and immediately closed the distance before the man could ready another strike. Grabbing the attacker's stick-wielding arm, Vik trapped it in an elbow lock while simultaneously gripping the stick with his free hand. A sharp tug disarmed the man, sending the stick's momentum into the attacker's head.

The entire fight lasted less than thirty seconds.

The first man, recovering from Vik's initial sidekick, staggered and glared at him. 'You don't know who sent us or what he's capable of,' he growled.

Vik's expression was calm but steely. 'Give Badal Gupta my regards,' he said coldly. 'Now get out of here while you can still walk.'

The four men didn't need to be told twice. Without a second glance, they melted into the shadows. Vik turned and gestured for me to come down. I stopped recording and hurried to join him.

'Let's get a cab before they come back with reinforcements,' Vik muttered, his pace brisk as we headed for the main road.

'That was incredible,' I blurted out, still buzzing with adrenaline. 'I've never seen you fight like that before.'

'That's Krav Maga,' Vik replied. 'It's what I'm studying these days.'

As we climbed into a cab, Vik's expression darkened, his thoughts racing, 'Badal Gupta is getting desperate to protect Nahar. His men must have seen us at the crime scene and followed. They might have recognized me. Badal knows my police connections and wants to rattle me. But in his panic over my involvement, he's made a foolish move.'

'Shouldn't we warn Avay?' I asked.

'Definitely. He might be targeted too.' Vik's voice was firm. 'Rik, upload the video to every social media platform you can think of. Let's expose these thugs and their master.'

'What caption should I use?' I asked, opening the app.

Vik thought for a moment. A faint smirk crossed his face. 'Instant karma for a minister's goons.'

***

After dinner, Vik was engrossed in his tablet, scrolling through videos with a casual focus. I'd been holding back something for a while, but now seemed a time to speak up. 'Something doesn't sit right about Harinath's death,' I said, trying to keep my tone casual but firm. 'Everything points to Nahar, but... it feels off.'

Vik glanced up, intrigued. 'Go on.'

I leaned forward, attempting to piece my thoughts together. 'Nahar's a professional criminal, right? He's committed countless crimes but has never been convicted. So how does someone that careful leave the murder weapon at the scene? It doesn't add up.'

Vik smirked faintly, tapping his fingers on the armrest. 'Nice observation. So, tell me, Rik—if not Nahar, then who?'

I hesitated but eventually said what had been on my mind. 'Ranadip. He's the sole heir to his father's fortune, right? Who knows how desperately he needed the money.'

Vik raised an eyebrow, intrigued but sceptical. 'Alright, say it was Ranadip. How and when did he do it? The shopkeeper was there the whole time. He said no one had entered for an hour after Nahar had left. And Harinath was alive when Nahar went inside.'

'Maybe Ranadip came back much earlier than he claimed. After Nahar left, he could've sneaked into the house by scaling the wall through the park, killed his father, and left the same way. Later, he came in through the front gate and pretended to find the body.'

Vik shook his head, unconvinced. 'The park was crowded, Rik. People would've noticed him scaling the wall. The other sides of the house have neighbours. He'd have to be crazy to risk being seen.'

I persisted, 'Then maybe he did it when he got home at 6:30. He could've murdered his father and started screaming right after.'

Vik chuckled softly, a touch of amusement in his tone, 'Even worse. A post-mortem would easily reveal the time of death. Ranadip's whole act would crumble.'

'Fine,' I admitted, growing frustrated. 'What about the army doctor? Dr Rana could've done it for the money. Maybe Harinath cheated him while investing his savings in the share market.'

Vik leaned back, his expression thoughtful but cautious, 'Interesting theory. But without evidence, it's just speculation.

And remember, not every case has a twist. Sometimes, the obvious answer is the right one. Maybe Nahar did kill Harinath. Go to bed, Rik. It's late.'

He returned to his tablet, the conversation over. I stole a glance at the screen as I stood up. He was watching a YouTube video on cardiopulmonary resuscitation—CPR. Vik had a habit of watching medical videos to expand his general knowledge. It seemed he wasn't as troubled by the case as I was, convinced that Nahar was the culprit.

But the unease gnawed at me. Something about Harinath's murder didn't add up.

Before heading to bed, I checked the video of Vik's fight. To my amazement, it had already crossed one million views.

***

Avay called around 11 am the next day. Vik put the phone on a loudspeaker so I could listen in.

'Hi, Victor. What have you done? You're the new internet sensation!' Avay's voice sounded equal parts amused and astonished.

'Really?' Vik replied, his tone casual.

'Oh, yes. Your fighting video has gone viral. The man who pointed the gun at you is Dipu Mondal, a known associate of Badal Gupta. He's been spotted alongside Badal multiple times during election campaigns. Now, the minister is scrambling. This morning, he gave a public statement claiming he's not associated with Dipu and has no connections to Nahar. He's blaming the opposition for using dirty tricks to defame him before the elections. In short, Nahar's been officially disavowed—he's on his own now.'

'That's great news,' Vik said.

'All thanks to your video.'

Vik shot me a thumbs-up, his face lighting up with a rare smile of appreciation.

'And there's more,' Avay continued, his excitement evident. 'We've got Nahar's fingerprint on the murder weapon. This seals the deal—no one can save him now. At the very least, he'll get life imprisonment. We'll push for the death penalty. Let's see how it goes.'

'What's Nahar saying?' Vik asked, his tone laced with curiosity.

'He's denying it, of course. Claims he didn't kill Harinath.' Avay let out a short laugh. 'Who's going to believe him?'

'What about the post-mortem report?' Vik pressed.

'Nothing unexpected,' Avay replied. 'The cause of death is mentioned as excessive blood loss due to the cut in the neck. His heart is also found to be damaged like he had a massive heart attack. The forensic doctor said this is natural in severe blood loss, particularly if the person already has a weak heart. Rib fractures are also there, which we were already aware of.'

'I see,' Vik murmured, his expression thoughtful. 'Congratulations on your success. About that address I asked for in the text—can you send it to me now?'

'Yes, I saw it. What is it for?'

'It's personal,' Vik replied, keeping his tone light. 'Nothing to do with the case.'

There was a brief pause before Avay said, 'Alright. I'll send it over. And thank you for everything—you've been a tremendous help.'

'Most welcome,' Vik said, ending the call.

He stared at his phone screen for a moment, his expression unreadable. A message tone chimed. Without a word, Vik stood and pocketed his phone.

'Get ready, Rik,' he said briskly. 'We're going out.'

'Where to?' I asked, unable to suppress my curiosity.

'No questions,' Vik said, already heading toward the door.

***

We reached New Town again in no time. Vik directed the cab driver while checking the GPS on his phone. I dared not ask any questions. This time, we didn't go to the murder site. Instead, the cab stopped before a standalone flat in the same neighbourhood.

'Second floor, Rik. Let's go,' Vik said as he stepped out of the cab.

He rang the doorbell of a second-floor flat. Dr. Siddharth Rana answered, dressed in a crisp white kurta-pajama and a grey shawl over his shoulders.

'You?' Dr. Rana's surprise was evident.

I was taken aback, having no clue why we were here.

'Sorry to disturb you, sir,' Vik said politely. 'I'll only need fifteen minutes of your time.'

'Please, come in.'

The living room was immaculate, its neatness reflecting a disciplined mind. A modest sofa set surrounded a polished centre table. Bookshelves lined one wall, and a display cabinet gleamed with medals and plaques—tangible evidence of Dr. Rana's illustrious career.

'How can I help you?' Dr. Rana asked as we sat down.

Vik leaned forward slightly. 'Sir, I hope you can answer a few questions about cardiopulmonary resuscitation.'

For a brief moment, Dr Rana's composed expression wavered, his face growing stern. 'What do you mean?'

Vik's tone hardened. 'I know how your friend died—and, more importantly, what happened afterwards.'

Dr Rana's eyes narrowed as he sat across from Vik. His voice dropped to a stone-cold register. 'What do you think you know?'

My heart was pounding by now, but Vik remained unruffled. 'Let me elaborate on yesterday evening's events,' he said calmly. 'Of course, there's some guesswork involved, so feel free to correct me if I'm wrong.'

'I'm listening,' Dr. Rana replied, his tone measured.

'You were at Harinath's house yesterday afternoon, long before Nahar arrived. You and Harinath were drinking together in the ground-floor bedroom. When Nahar showed up, you were already there. Here's where I'll speculate. While Harinath went to answer the door, you stepped into the washroom. From there, you overheard the entire confrontation. Nahar likely threatened Harinath as soon as the door opened, prompting Harinath to retreat to the bedroom and seek your support. However, Nahar never saw you because you chose to stay hidden in the washroom—why did you do so? Only you can explain. Yet, through the slightly ajar bathroom door, you witnessed everything. Nahar didn't come to kill; he came only to threaten Harinath about his son. Unfortunately, he picked up the knife from the fruit platter to be more intimidating. That single, impulsive act was the mistake that ultimately sealed his fate.'

'Are you accusing me of murder?' Dr Rana's voice was tight with controlled anger. 'Why would I kill my friend?'

'I never said you killed anyone,' Vik replied. 'Let me finish. Harinath wasn't killed at all—he died of natural causes. His weak heart gave out under the stress of Nahar's threats, and he had a massive heart attack right after Nahar left. You tried to save him using CPR but failed. You checked him and understood that he was already dead, and there was no point in calling an ambulance. Then the righteous soldier in you woke up, and you decided not to let your friend's death remain in vain. Am I right?'

Dr Rana's silence was telling, but his face betrayed nothing.

'Now,' Vik continued, his voice even, 'let's talk about CPR. Correct me if I'm mistaken. Cardiopulmonary resuscitation is the basic life support procedure for a person who has suffered cardiac arrest or whose heart has stopped. It involves chest compressions using palm and mouth-to-mouth breathing. Chest compressions artificially pump blood through the body even after the heart has stopped. If the person is still alive, these actions can eventually restart the heart, reviving them. However, forceful chest compressions often result in rib fractures, especially in older individuals. Understood, Rik?' Vik looked at me.

I nodded.

Vik continued, 'Now if you cut the throat of a dead person, blood would ooze out very slowly because the heart is no longer pumping. This would be evident during a forensic examination. But what if you cut the throat of someone who has just died and then performed chest compressions on them?'

I began to understand. 'The blood would spurt as if the person were alive, making it seem like the throat injury was the cause of death even though they were already dead.'

'Exactly. Even forensic doctors would be deceived, concluding that the heart attack was secondary to massive blood loss from the throat injury. Now, let's revisit the scene. You decided Nahar should be punished. So, you removed all your clothes and, wearing gloves from your medical kit, sliced your dead friend's throat using the same knife Nahar had touched. Then, you performed chest compressions on him, forcing the blood to flow in spurts and creating a gruesome crime scene. Afterwards, you had to bathe to clean off the blood but didn't notice a drop of it dripping near the bathroom door. After cleaning yourself and putting your clothes back on, you needed to eliminate all evidence of your presence. You emptied the alcohol glasses in the sink but forgot to wash them, leaving a faint smell of alcohol in two of the glasses and the sink itself.

'You couldn't leave the house immediately because the shop across the street had reopened, and the shopkeeper would have noticed you going through the front gate. Escaping through the garden wasn't an option either, as people in the park would have spotted you. So, you hid in the garden instead. Taking a bath in the evening and standing outside in the cold winter air gave you a cold, which is why you were sneezing during our conversation. The mosquito bites on your hands and face also gave you away. When Ranadip arrived and discovered the body, onlookers and neighbours started gathering. The shopkeeper became distracted, and people began entering the garden. You seized this opportunity to blend into the crowd, making it appear as though you had just arrived. That's the entire sequence. Did I miss anything?'

Dr Rana sighed deeply, his voice calm. 'You've told your story. But can you prove it?'

'I don't want to,' Vik replied. 'The only person responsible for Harinath's death is Nahar. He deserves to pay for his crimes. Your actions, however extreme, came from a sense of duty to justice.'

Dr Rana's expression softened with gratitude. 'Thank you.'

'I have just one question,' Vik said. 'Why didn't you step out of the bathroom when Nahar threatened Harinath? You could have helped him.'

Dr Rana's shoulders sagged slightly. 'It was clear Nahar didn't intend to attack. I thought it better to stay hidden. Confronting him might have escalated things. Still, I couldn't save my friend.'

A heavy silence filled the room.

Finally, Vik rose to his feet. 'You did what you believed was right, and for that, you have my respect. We'll take our leave now.'

As we headed for the door, Dr. Rana called, 'Why did you come here to tell me all this if you didn't intend to reveal it?'

Vik chuckled, 'I had to confirm my deductions. I never leave a case unsolved.'

The Deadly Gambit

'So, what's going to be the main attraction tomorrow?' Samrat asked, leaning back in his chair.

'Cocktails, of course. And I've hired a dance troupe,' Rajit replied confidently.

'That's at every party. We need something fresh,' Jayant demanded with a hint of impatience.

Rajit snapped, 'What else do you expect at a housewarming party?'

Mayank chimed in, 'Isn't Victor coming tomorrow?'

'The detective?' Harsh asked, raising an eyebrow.

'He's not a detective; he says it's just a hobby,' Bhaskar corrected.

'Whatever he is, let's give him a surprise tomorrow. That'll be fun,' proposed Samrat, his eyes glinting with mischief.

'What kind of surprise?' Jayant asked curiously.

Samrat grinned. 'Let's give him a case to solve.'

'A case? Like what?' Harsh pressed.

Samrat leaned forward conspiratorially, 'A murder, maybe.'

'Are you out of your mind?' Mayank exclaimed, shaking his head.

'I mean a fake murder,' Samrat clarified, undeterred.

'Not a bad idea,' Jayant admitted. 'But we'll have to fool him by acting.'

'But who's going to play the dead body?' Rajit asked, crossing his arms.

'Bhaskar, of course,' Samrat declared with a chuckle.

'No way. I can't do this,' Bhaskar protested immediately.

Before anyone could argue further, the telephone rang. Rajit picked it up, his face falling as he listened, 'Bad news, folks. Victor can't come tomorrow. He has to attend a seminar.'

'What the…!' Samrat exclaimed, visibly deflated. 'That ruins all the fun.'

'Not entirely,' Mayank said. 'We can still enjoy ourselves, even without Victor.'

'Thank God,' Bhaskar muttered, relieved. 'At least I don't have to play the dead body.'

'But we will still play the game of death,' Samrat declared dramatically.

'The game of death?' the five voices chorused, leaning in with intrigue.

'Yes,' Samrat said with a grin. 'The game is simple. Have you heard of a poison called Aconite?'

'Aconite?' Harsh and Mayank echoed together. 'No, what is it?'

'It's a herbal poison,' Samrat explained, 'You can mix it with a drink in powdered form. It dissolves easily and tastes sweet so that no one will suspect it. Once consumed, it attacks the heart. Death is inevitable.'

'Are you out of your mind?' Rajit exclaimed, his voice rising. 'You're not seriously considering using something that dangerous, are you? I don't want any accidents at my housewarming party!'

'Relax,' Samrat said with a laugh. 'We'll use glucose powder instead. Just imagine it's Aconite. We will carry a small packet of glucose powder folded in paper. Once the game starts, the goal is simple: mix your glucose into someone else's glass without being noticed. When someone drinks it, they're considered "dead" and out of the game. They'll immediately hand their glass to the bartender and stop drinking for the night. The last person standing—"alive"—wins. How does that sound?'

'Awesome!' Jayant shouted, clapping his hands. 'It'll be great fun. Let's play it.'

'But the girls will be there too,' Harsh pointed out.

'That's not a problem,' Samrat said dismissively. 'They can enjoy themselves their way. We'll enjoy ourselves our way.'

Everyone nodded in agreement.

'It's a shame Victor won't come,' Rajit sighed. 'He would've loved this game.'

'He doesn't drink,' Harsh replied. 'And there's no mystery in it anyway; it's just a game.'

'By the way, what's on the menu?' Mayank asked, changing the subject.

'You don't need to worry about that,' Harsh said confidently. 'Rajit put me in charge of it, and I hired the best caterer in Kolkata. It's all sorted.'

'That's what I'd be worried about,' Samrat quipped, smirking.

The room erupted in laughter.

***

The next evening, the party was about to begin. Rajit and his wife Nandini were welcoming the guests. With no relatives in Kolkata, all the attendees were friends.

Jayant and Mayank arrived with their wives, Nisha and Anamika. Another girl, Reena, was Harsh's best friend.

Samrat was brimming with excitement for the game. He handed each player a small paper pouch of glucose powder, grinning mischievously. The bartender stood ready, whiskey bottles glinting under the dim light. Rajit said, 'Let the dance troupe arrive first. Then we'll begin the game.'

Bhaskar suddenly pulled Harsh aside and said, 'Harsh, please do me a favour. I want to propose to Reena today. You know how much I love her.'

Harsh raised an eyebrow. 'Everyone knows. But let's face it, Bhaskar, you don't have the guts to propose. You've been trying for four years! And you know she's into Samrat.'

'Samrat flirts. That's all. He'll never marry her, and you know it. You're her best friend. Do you want to see her with someone like Samrat or someone who truly loves her?'

Harsh sighed, rubbing his temple. 'You're right. Samrat will never marry her. Fine. I'll talk to her and arrange a moment for you two. But listen carefully: you'll have to do it yourself. If you chicken out today, I'm done helping you.'

'Okay. Just set it up. I'll handle the rest,' Bhaskar said, his desperation evident.

The dance troupe arrived at seven sharp, and the game began. The girls chose not to participate, leaving six players. Each took a whiskey-filled glass wrapped in tissue paper from the bartender.

The room resembled a nightclub, with dim lights and a stage set for the dancers. The troupe positioned themselves at one end, ready to perform.

Samrat addressed the group, his voice commanding. 'One more rule: no changing glasses. If you want a refill, use the same glass. Once you're out, deposit your glass with the bartender. You can enjoy the dance and food, but no more drinks tonight. Once "dead," you're done. The bartender's been briefed—he won't serve you. Everyone clear?'

The others nodded.

'Let the game begin.'

Right then, someone's elbow sent a pouch skittering to the floor. Harsh stooped to pick it up, holding it between two fingers as if it were something faintly distasteful. He dusted it off with exaggerated care, then handed it to Mayank, smirking. 'Here you go, Mayank. Try not to poison anyone too early—save it for the game.'

'Careful, Harsh,' Mayank said with a faint smirk as he slipped the pouch into his pocket. 'You might regret handing this over.'

Mayank's smirk lingered as the group settled back into their places, the game's tension thickening around them. The first round passed without incident. Each player tried to outwit the others, but no one succeeded. Bhaskar, however, seemed distracted, glancing at his glass as if lost in thought, though he managed to survive.

As the glasses were refilled. Bhaskar's absent-mindedness became more pronounced. Samrat seized the moment, emptying his pouch into Bhaskar's drink. Bhaskar took a long sip.

'Dea-a-a-d!' the players chorused, grinning as Bhaskar grimaced. Reluctantly, he handed his glass to the bartender and joined the girls, following the rules. Though he tried to focus on the dance show, his thoughts were elsewhere.

The game pressed on. Harsh was the next to fall. He had played well initially but became distracted by the belly dancers after Bhaskar's dismissal. Jayant pounced on the opportunity.

Harsh looked incredulous, 'What? Me? How?'

Samrat chuckled, 'Your fault, mate. No one distracted you—you did it to yourself. Now, deposit your glass and enjoy belly dancing to your heart's content. Want me to set you up with one of them?'

Harsh scowled, 'Stop your nonsense, Samrat. I know the rules. I'll check on the catering.'

Leaving his glass with the bartender, Harsh marched into the next room, muttering.

'Poor Harsh,' Samrat quipped, shaking his head. 'Such a

devoted drinker, yet out of the game so soon. Tragic. Right, four left! Let's keep going.'

Jayant and Mayank soon met their fate, distracted by Samrat's clever chatter. Rajit eliminated Jayant, while Samrat took out Mayank. Both were visibly annoyed, grumbling about their thirst.

Now, it was down to two: Rajit and Samrat. The tension rose as the pair matched wits, neither giving an inch. Finally, Rajit faltered, distracted by Nandini's arrival. She began discussing household matters, and Samrat seized his chance. The game was over.

Samrat declared triumphantly, 'Winner, at last!'

Harsh returned to the hall and announced, 'Come on, everyone. Dinner is ready.'

The guests gradually went to the dining room, where the dinner table was set. Harsh whispered something to Reena, who then walked to the front door. Nandini asked, 'Won't you have dinner, Reena?'

'I'm not hungry right now. Besides, Harsh will drop me home, so I'm in no hurry. I'll eat later with you all. I need some fresh air,' Reena replied.

Everyone except Rajit, Nandini, Harsh, and Reena sat for dinner. Harsh monitored the catering. Rajit and Nandini were busy with other tasks. Reena waited outside.

After a while, Harsh went outside and returned to Bhaskar, whispering, 'This is your moment. Reena's waiting for you outside. Go now.'

Bhaskar froze for a second, then sprang to his feet, leaving a half-eaten bowl of ice cream behind. Harsh escorted him to the hall, now deserted, murmuring words of encouragement. At the threshold, Harsh pointed toward the garden.

'All the best. You know what to do,' Harsh said before returning to the dining room.

Bhaskar took his time and slowly marched in the garden towards Reena. He felt numb, and his throat dried. 'I have to do it today,' he said to himself. Reena was standing with her back to Bhaskar. He called her from behind, and she looked back. She was smiling. 'I wanted to talk to you, Reena,' Bhaskar began.

'Yes, Bhaskar. What is it?'

Reena waited. She knew what he wanted to say and already knew her answer.

'I…I…I…,' Bhaskar stammered.

Reena thought, 'Typical Bhaskar. Can't even propose confidently.' But she remained silent, waiting.

'I…I…,' Bhaskar tried again, his face contorted.

'Yes, Bhaskar. Tell me what you want to say.'

Bhaskar grimaced further. 'Whenever I think of you, whenever I see you…ah…my mouth burns.'

'What? I think you mean your heart burns,' Reena said, startled.

'My heart is burning too. Sorry, Reena. I'll be back in five minutes.'

Without waiting for her response, Bhaskar rushed back into the house, leaving Reena taken aback.

Ten minutes passed, but Bhaskar didn't return.

When Harsh returned to the dining room, Rajit announced, 'Good news. Victor is coming. He just called—his seminar is over. He'll be here any moment.'

'Really? That's great. If he'd come earlier, he would've loved the game,' Samrat said.

A sudden scream pierced the air as the first batch of guests finished dinner and chatted. It was a woman's voice coming from the bathroom.

They rushed to the source and froze in horror. Bhaskar lay

sprawled on the floor, the faucet gushing water. Reena crouched in a corner, hands covering her face. Rajit knelt beside Bhaskar, checking his pulse. Slowly, he shook his head, his face pale.

'He's dead,' Rajit whispered.

At that moment, Victor walked into the house.

***

Inspector Rishav Ganguly examined the body with meticulous care while the forensic team had already begun their work.

He turned to a young member of the forensic team and asked, 'What do you think is the cause of death?'

'Poison, sir. But the exact nature will only be confirmed after the autopsy.'

It had been a long and taxing day for Rishav. Just as he was preparing to head home, another homicide case came in, with orders from higher authorities to attend it personally. Naturally, his mood was far from pleasant.

As per his instructions to the house owner, no one was allowed to leave until he arrived. The guests, therefore, remained in the house and gathered in the hall.

One face in the group caught Rishav's attention. It looked familiar. The man was standing in a corner, slightly apart from the rest.

Rishav approached him, 'Are you Victor Chatterjee?'

'Yes. How do you know me?'

'I trained with your friend Avay at the academy. He told me about how you helped him in a few cases. He spoke highly of you. He even mentioned you once acted as a spy for the Indian Government,' Rishav lowered his voice as he said the last sentence.

Victor shifted uncomfortably, 'Not at all. Avay exaggerates. It wasn't anything like that.'

'Well, it's good you're here. I'd like to hear your perspective on this case. But, of course, I'll need to verify your alibi first.'

'Of course. I'll provide the details of the seminar I was attending,' Victor took out his phone, opened an image, and handed it to Rishav.

Rishav straightened and said, 'I'll be interrogating each of you in the next room, one by one. Victor, you're first.'

As Victor followed Rishav, Jayant muttered, 'What a strange officer! He wants to interrogate someone who knows nothing about the incident first.'

'I think he wants Victor's help to solve the case,' Mayank replied.

'So now Victor is going to interrogate us?' Jayant said, his irritation evident.

Harsh, overhearing them, interjected, 'Guys, please. Our friend has been murdered. Whatever it takes, we need to catch the killer.'

Samrat, who had been silent since the body was discovered, remained visibly shaken by the incident.

Soon, Rajit's turn was to be interrogated. When he entered the room, he was surprised to find Victor seated beside Rishav.

Rishav spoke first, 'Victor has agreed to assist the police in solving the case. He wants to ensure the murderer of his friend is brought to justice. Please answer his questions as well.'

Rajit, though slightly annoyed, nodded.

Rishav began by asking Rajit formal questions about his background and the other guests, particularly their whereabouts. He then asked Rajit to describe the evening's events in detail. Once Rajit finished, Rishav turned to Victor.

Victor leaned forward slightly and asked, 'You mentioned the game earlier. I need you to recount what happened during the game in the exact order. Who dismissed whom, and how?'

Both Rajit and Rishav stared at him, startled by the question. Rajit felt his irritation rising. To him, the query seemed irrelevant—everyone knew who had eliminated Bhaskar in the game, and Inspector Rishav had already been briefed. What could possibly be the relevance of who dismissed the others?

Rajit waited, hoping Rishav would dismiss the question, but the inspector remained silent, apparently deferring to Victor. Reluctantly, Rajit began recounting the details of the game. As he spoke, Rishav stifled a yawn, but Victor listened intently, his expression thoughtful.

When Rajit emerged from the makeshift interrogation room, he leaned toward Harsh and whispered, 'We're all so shaken by Bhaskar's death, and here Victor is, making fun of us in front of the police. What a terrible evening this is turning out to be!'

***

Samrat frowned as Victor asked his first question, 'Do you love Reena?'

'Don't you think it is too personal a question?' He retorted.

'I think not answering questions will not help you,' Victor replied calmly.

Samrat was taken aback at his reply. He pondered and replied, 'Listen, I am a careerist. So, I don't want to get involved in something that will hinder my career growth. Reena is a good friend. But I have never thought beyond that.'

'Is she aware of this?'

'Of course. I have told her several times that I don't want anything serious.'

Rishav asked, 'We know you poured something into Bhaskar's

glass during the game. What do you want to say about that?'

'Come on, that was glucose powder. Everyone had it. That was part of the game.'

Rishav smirked, 'Glucose can also be replaced with something else. Anyway, once the forensic report from the whiskey glasses is available, we'll know more. Meanwhile, you can rest assured if you haven't done anything.'

Samrat left the room with a grim face.

Harsh was next.

After Rishav's questions, Victor asked, 'You arranged the catering. Can you tell me the menu?'

Rishav was a bit annoyed this time. It was hard to believe that this stupid man had solved those complex cases he had heard about. What the hell was he asking?

Harsh answered, 'We had chicken and vegetarian starters with the drinks. The main menu started with bread and curry, fish fry, fried rice, chicken and mutton dishes and one vegetable curry for vegetarians. This was followed by desserts, sweets, ice cream and pan masala as a mouth freshener.

To Rishav's relief, Victor asked something relevant, 'When you escorted Bhaskar to meet Reena, did you notice any abnormality in him? I mean any distress or sickness.'

'Well, he was nervous. His hands were shaking. I thought that was because he was going to propose. Apart from that, nothing else.'

'Ok. The last question, do you like belly dancing?'

Harsh's face twitched in disgust.

Rishav interfered, 'No need to answer that. You can go. Send Jayant, inside.'

Harsh came outside and told Rajit, 'You were right. Victor is being a pain in the ...' The last word was inaudible.

Before Jayant entered, Rishav warned Victor, 'I request that you keep your questions relevant to the case only. Please don't waste my time.'

Victor gently apologised.

Jayant was a bulky guy. However, he sat in a relaxed and idle manner.

Rishav asked, 'What were you doing after being out of the game?'

'Mayank and I went outside to drink some more. We managed the bartender to give us a bottle and took two plastic glasses. Why should we stop drinking for such a stupid game?'

Victor asked, 'Anyone saw you drinking outside?'

'No, there was no one outside. My wife might have guessed it, though.'

'What was Bhaskar doing then?'

'How would I know? I told you we were outside.'

Mayank seemed to be a little irritated when he entered.

Rishav asked, 'You went outside to drink with Jayant?'

'Does that make me a murderer?' He retorted.

'I never said that. Being hostile with me will not help you.' Rishav's tone was severe.

'What was Bhaskar doing then?' Victor asked.

'That idiot! He was flirting with my wife.'

'Are you sure? Can anyone do that just before proposing to another girl?'

'Is it? Then why was he whispering constantly with Anamika?'

Rishav asked, 'Did you feel angry seeing this?'

'Not enough to kill him,' Mayank quipped.

Victor asked, 'If you were outside drinking with Jayant, how did you notice all these things?'

Mayank hesitated, then grunted, fixing Victor with a sharp look.

'Also, Mayank,' Victor said, his tone casual but his gaze sharp, 'you were the one who dropped your pouch during the game, weren't you?'

Mayank's jaw tightened. 'What does that have to do with anything?' he replied curtly, his eyes narrowing slightly.

Rishav let out a quiet sigh, the frustration evident on his face. This interrogation was going nowhere.

'Let's call the ladies now,' He declared.

Nandini was the first to come.

Rishav asked, 'How was Bhaskar's relation with his friends?'

Nandini replied sadly, 'All of them, including my hubby, used to bully him. Jayant and Mayank were the worst. Only Victor used to support him.'

Victor nodded.

Rishav asked, 'Had any of them quarrelled with Bhaskar recently?'

'Bhaskar was a nice guy. He never raised his voice in front of anyone. Rather, Rajit had a recent quarrel with Jayant. But that is unrelated.'

Victor asked, 'We still want to know about it. What was the quarrel about?'

'Jayant almost begged Rajit to invest in his start-up business. So Rajit gave him a lump sum. But he lost all the money within a short time. Both quarrelled over the phone about this a few days before. I heard Rajit saying that he would get the money back with the help of his police friends.'

Victor remarked, 'That is quite serious, but that doesn't explain why anyone would kill Bhaskar.'

Nandini suddenly realised something that made her shudder, 'What if Bhaskar was not the target?'

Both Victor and Rishav were startled.

Victor said, 'Don't confuse me, Nandini. I am a simple person. I can't think too complicated.'

Rishav waved her to go. Jayant's wife, Nisha, was the next to enter.

Rishav asked, 'Did you notice any change in Bhaskar after he was out of the game?'

'Anamika was flirting with him. But he seemed to be unmindful.'

'Anamika was flirting? And Mayank thinks it was Bhaskar.'

'Huh! As if he doesn't know that his wife is friendly with everyone.'

'What about you? Have you been friendly with any one of them?' Rishav regretted asking the question. It seemed inappropriate.

The answer was even more uncomfortable, 'Ask the person sitting by you. He knows that I have always loved him. But he has always remained ignorant while living in his world.'

A deadly silence fell in the room after Nisha left. Victor seemed to be embarrassed.

Anamika came next.

Rishav asked, 'People are complaining that you flirt with boys. What do you want to say about this?'

Anamika guffawed, 'They are jealous. The boys are after me. Now, I am a friendly and down-to-earth person. That is not flirting. Right, Victor?'

Anamika looked at Victor with a sidelong glance while saying this.

Victor asked, 'What was Bhaskar telling you?'

'He was nervous. He wanted to propose to Reena but was unable to gather enough courage. So, I was helping him out.'

'Did you two have dinner together?'

'Yes. Bhaskar was sitting with me only.'

'Did he finish his food before Harsh called him?'

'He had almost finished. He just left the half-eaten ice cream.'

'Wasn't there any other food item served after this?'

'Oh, only this.' Anamika lifted a plastic ziplock pouch filled with pan masala, which she held with her handkerchief.

Rishav was in a hurry as Victor was again going away from the context, 'Okay. Send Reena, in.'

A dead silence prevailed outside in the living room. All the guests were still waiting. Discontent was writ large on their faces.

Victor asked Reena, 'Are you sure that he said his mouth burns?'

'Yes, of course.'

'What was he looking like then?'

'It was dark. I couldn't take a good look. But it seemed he was in pain. And the next moment, he was running to the house.'

'What did you do then?'

'I was puzzled. I thought he had a nervous breakdown. After a while, I went inside to search for him. I heard the sound of tap water flowing from the washroom. And…' Reena covered her face.

'Were there water splashes on Bhaskar's face when you discovered him?'

'I don't remember. It was a horrible scene. I couldn't bear to look.'

Rishav said, 'Probably he was washing his face. Some poisons cause burning of the eyes and mouth when they start working. Anyway, you can go.'

Victor remained seated unmindfully.

After Reena left, Rishav said, 'We should interrogate the catering staff now.'

Victor returned to his senses, 'Yes, let's start with the bartender serving alcohol during the game.'

The bartender's name was Ramesh. He came, saluted both and sat hesitantly.

Victor asked, 'Did Jayant and Mayank ask for an extra whiskey bottle?'

Ramesh lowered his eyes, 'Yes, sir. They gave me money for it.'

'Why didn't you clean the glasses after the game?'

'Sir, we had a staff shortage. Harsh sir told me they needed extra hands in the kitchen. So, after the game, I went immediately to the kitchen.'

'Where was Harsh then?'

'In the kitchen. He remained there after he got out of the game until the dinner was ready.'

'Where were the others?'

'Sir, they talked in the same living room after the games. Then, once dinner was announced, they went to the dining room next to it.'

'And who was in the living room then?'

'I guess no one, sir.'

'So, you forgot about the glasses.'

'I didn't forget, sir. I was going to clean them after the last batch of dinner. But before that….'

'The glasses were found nicely wrapped in tissue papers. Did you serve them like this?'

'Yes, sir, as they were chilled.'

'Hmmm. You can go.'

Once Ramesh left, Victor asked Rishav, 'Did you send the glasses to the forensic lab?

'Of course. As you know, you can't expect to find fingerprints as the glasses were wrapped. Lip prints may be found, though.'

Victor smirked, 'I guess you won't get those too.'

Rishav was a bit confused at this and was going to say something.

But Victor asked again, 'What about toxicology?'

'Oh, you know. A toxicology report may take a long time, even a month or more. But this is a high-profile case. Your friend Rajit has connections in headquarters. So, I'll try to get an interim report. Anyway, the postmortem report will be ready by tomorrow.'

'Tell them to check for Aconite. It will be fast if they know which poison to search for.'

'Why Aconite? It can be any other poison.'

'Just a thought. The murderer might have used the same poison pretended to be used in the game. Well, I'll take your leave now, if you allow me. You can finish interrogating the rest of the staff. Please let me know once you get your interim report.'

'Surely. But could you make anything out of the interrogation so far? Do you have any idea who the killer is?'

Victor shook his head slightly, 'Too early to comment.'

Rishav leaned back thoughtfully, 'I think Nandini may have had a point. Rajit might have been the real target. He's the wealthiest of them all. We've assumed this is about a woman, but maybe it's about money. I'll dig deeper to see if Jayant desperately needs cash.'

'That sounds reasonable. Continue investigating as you see fit,' Victor replied. Then, after a pause, he added, 'But I strongly recommend you post a constable outside the house 24x7. I suspect further unlawful activities may occur.'

Rishav frowned at the suggestion but eventually nodded.

The guests were still in the living room. Victor wished them good night and went out of the house. He waited on the threshold, his eyes searching for something.

Soon, he found what he was searching for. A small object lying on the grass was quickly located as it reflected light.

***

The next day, Victor received a call from Rishav around 4 pm.

Rishav sounded excited as he spoke, 'Hi, Victor. I'm calling to let you know that the case has been solved. I've just arrested the murderer. You were right about the poison—the forensic team found Aconite in Bhaskar's stomach and one of the whiskey glasses. It's now pretty obvious who did it. Samrat is already in police custody.'

'Where did you arrest him? At his house?'

'No, at Rajit's house. They're all gathered there, discussing what happened yesterday.'

'All of them?'

'Everyone, except Reena.'

'Has Samrat said anything?'

'He's only asked for his lawyer.'

'Are you still there?'

'Yes, but I'm about to leave.'

'I need a favour from you. Please listen carefully.'

A short while later, Rishav entered the living room at Rajit's house with an annoyed face. All the previous evening's guests, except Reena and Samrat, were present. Samrat had already been taken to the police van.

Rishav addressed the group, 'Listen, everyone. Your friend Victor is a crackpot. He still believes Samrat is innocent and wants to search the garden tomorrow morning for some 'evidence', which he claims will turn the case upside down. He's even requested a constable to stay here until then. Frankly, I think it's a waste of time and manpower. But because of his connections, I can't ignore him completely.'

He sighed and continued, 'I'll let him run his little errand tomorrow morning, but I can only spare a constable until midnight—no longer. I hope that's not a problem, Rajit.'

Rajit replied confidently, 'Of course not, officer. Samrat's guilt is proven beyond doubt. You can remove the police posting now if you want.'

Rishav smirked, 'I still have a job to keep, bro. Your detective friend has influence in the highest places. So, the constable stays until midnight—but don't tell Victor. Can I trust you all to keep this a secret?'

Everyone nodded in agreement.

'Good. And now that the case is solved, you're free to go wherever you wish.'

With that, Rishav left the house in a hurry.

***

The lights in the house turned off at midnight. The garden was now deserted.

Victor slowly made his way toward Rajit's house, stopping on the footpath opposite it. Moments later, Rishav and two constables emerged from the nearest alley.

Victor asked, 'Did you bring what I asked for?'

Rishav nodded. 'Yes—a walkie-talkie with a Bluetooth headset. We'll communicate through this. Here's your earpiece. I've also got an action camera to record everything for evidence.'

Victor looked satisfied, 'Perfect. Let's take our positions behind those big trees in the garden. And remember—not a single move until I give the signal.'

The wait was long and unpleasant. Victor, having applied mosquito repellent cream, was relatively comfortable. Rishav and the constables, however, were not so fortunate.

Around 2 am, a hooded figure appeared in the garden, jumping over the wall with agility. It moved stealthily toward the front door but didn't enter the house. Instead, it began searching the garden for something. After a few tense minutes, the figure froze, seemingly having found what it was looking for.

As the figure bent down to pick up something from the grass, Victor whispered into the walkie-talkie, 'Now.'

All four men lunged forward simultaneously.

Rishav lit his torch and barked, 'Hands up!'

The figure was startled, but before it could react, the constables had seized it.

'Allow me to introduce you to the murderer,' Victor said, pulling back the hood in one swift motion. Even in the dim moonlight, the disgust on Harsh's face was unmistakable.

Rishav carefully took what Harsh had been clutching in his right hand—a ziplock plastic pouch.

'So, this is how the poison was administered,' Rishav said grimly.

Victor nodded. 'Yes, through pan masala. The pouch will test positive for aconite. Send it to the forensic lab.'

Harsh, stunned by the sudden arrest, stood speechless.

After the constables had taken him away, Victor pulled an envelope from his pocket and handed it to Rishav.

'The original pouch is inside this envelope. Replace the one Harsh just picked up with this before sending it to forensics. That one was planted by me just an hour ago.'

Rishav's eyes narrowed in confusion. 'But, how...?'

'I found the pouch that same evening. I didn't want to risk it being blown away by the wind, so I kept it safe. Don't worry—it contains aconite and has the fingerprints of both Harsh and Bhaskar. Now you've got video evidence as well. This will leave no room for doubt in proving Harsh guilty.'

Rishav stared at him, then extended his hand with gratitude, 'Thank you, Victor. You've saved an innocent man.'

***

The following day, everyone gathered at Rajit's house again for breakfast. Samrat, who had been released the previous night, was also present.

After breakfast, during tea, the group pressed Victor to share his thoughts on the case.

Victor began, 'One thing was clear to me from the beginning—the motive. But tell me, why were you all so quick to believe that Samrat was the murderer just because the poison was found in the whiskey glass?'

Rajit replied, 'We all thought Samrat somehow found out that Reena liked Bhaskar and would accept his proposal. So, out of jealousy, he killed him.'

'But the same reasoning could apply to Harsh,' Victor countered. 'He's Reena's best friend and secretly loves her. I believe he recently proposed to Reena and was rejected. Am I right, Reena?'

Reena nodded.

'When exactly did this happen?'

'A week before. I told him I could be only a friend, nothing more.'

Victor said, 'So the wound was fresh. After being friend-zoned, his jealousy of Samrat grew into wrath. Inspector Rishav hasn't received Harsh's statement yet—it might come later. Still, I believe I can reconstruct the crime with reasonable accuracy. Once the pieces of the puzzle come together, the story reveals itself. When Samrat planned the game for the housewarming party, Harsh acquired real Aconite poison and placed it in similar paper pouches. Initially, his plan may have been to target only Samrat. But before the game, Bhaskar confided in him about proposing to Reena, and Harsh realized she was interested in Bhaskar too. So, his wrath shifted to Bhaskar. How could a 'loser' like Bhaskar win Reena over him? Poor Bhaskar had no idea. The murder wasn't meticulously pre-planned. Harsh was looking for an opportunity to punish both Bhaskar and Samrat. He planned it instantly when the opportunity unfolded during the game. When Samrat dismissed Bhaskar from the game with glucose powder in his whiskey, Harsh quickly devised his plan. All he needed to do was spike one of the glasses with poison and ensure no one drank from it. It was simple—he pretended to be distracted by the belly dancer and deliberately got himself eliminated. Before returning his glass to the bartender, he mixed the poison in his glass. Now, the trap was set for Samrat. Harsh pretended to supervise catering and removed himself from the scene so that the least suspicion would fall on him. Have you ever heard of any guest spending the entire time in the kitchen supervising the catering as if he were serving food? When you try to be too clever, you make a fool of yourself. Anyway, Harsh knew exactly when he could poison Bhaskar. So, he didn't bother to come to the living room again. Of course, he had to call the bartender, telling him there was a staff shortage, so he wouldn't get time to clean the glasses. Otherwise, his trap for Samrat would have fallen apart. Once dinner was ready, he announced it to everyone in the hall. But he told Reena to wait outside in the garden as Bhaskar wanted to talk to her. That was a part of his plan. He then waited for the perfect moment to escort Bhaskar to the garden. When Bhaskar had nearly finished his meal, Harsh told him to meet Reena before the pan masala was served. Aconite is sweet, known as meetha zeher in Hindi, and its taste can easily be masked by pan masala. Harsh had a poisoned pan masala pouch, which he handed to Bhaskar while escorting him to the garden. He likely suggested Bhaskar freshen his mouth before proposing to Reena, perhaps even hinting at a kiss if she accepted. Poor Bhaskar took it and went to propose to Reena. Harsh left the garden, not wanting to be present when the poison took effect. He had one more task: smudging the lip prints on the glass brims so that it could not be proved that he had poisoned his glass. It took mere seconds, as the glasses were already there. He wiped the brims of all the glasses using a tissue, erasing the lip prints. He likely saw Bhaskar toss the ziplock pouch onto the grass but couldn't retrieve it in his presence. He planned to retrieve it later but lost the chance when I entered immediately after the incident. He couldn't risk collecting it while I was in the house. Before leaving, I ensured a 24x7 police presence at the house. He likely assumed no one would pay attention to an ordinary plastic pouch and would dismiss it. But yesterday, after Samrat was arrested, I baited him. Following my instructions, Rishav told all of you that I believed something in the garden could prove someone else's guilt. He added that the police posting would end at midnight. Harsh fell for the bait, returning to destroy the only evidence linking him to the crime—and was caught red-handed.'

'Excellent work, Victor.' Anamika said, 'But how did you solve the case?'

'Well, based on the motive, my suspicion fell on Harsh from the start. Secondly, those whiskey glasses were still lying on the table long after the game, and no one was in the room after the dinner was announced. Whoever the killer was had enough opportunity to eliminate the evidence by cleaning those glasses, yet he didn't do it. So, it crossed my mind that those glasses were just exhibited to pin the murder on someone else. The poison was given in some other way. Then there was Harsh's odd behaviour—getting distracted by a belly dancer and spending the entire party in the kitchen. This further solidified my suspicions. When I reviewed the menu and learned that Harsh had escorted Bhaskar to meet Reena just before the pan masala was served, I realized how the poisoning occurred. Reena, do you remember what Bhaskar told you? "My mouth burns." One of the first symptoms of Aconite poisoning is burning or numbness of the tongue, and usually, that happens immediately after ingestion, not an hour later. However, death can take up to an hour. But the burning begins as soon as the poison enters the mouth. Bhaskar was found with the tap water flowing as he washed his mouth, not his eyes or face. I understood that the ziplock pouch was the only thing which could prove Harsh guilty, and fortunately enough, I found it in the garden. I hope that now everything is clear to you.'

Samrat approached Victor, clasping his hands in gratitude. 'Thank you for saving me, Victor.'

Victor's expression grew sombre, 'The only regret is that we lost a good friend. Bhaskar will always be missed.'

A lone tear rolled down his cheek.

What Lies Beyond

'What are you watching, Rik? And who's that?' Vik tapped on my shoulder as I immersed myself in an online video on my smartphone.

With a spark of excitement, I replied, 'This is the Serpent Man, Chris Robinson. He's got this uncanny claim—he can tame any snake. Look at this! He performs live with wild snakes, their fangs intact. And the best part? He's in India now. This video is from Rajasthan, posted just last week.'

'An American snake charmer? Now, that's a twist. Forward me the link.'

'Sure,' I tapped the forward button. 'There you go.'

'I'll check it out later. Right now, a client's dropping by regarding a case. Rik, could you straighten up the living room? And please, move your game controller off the centre table.'

'A case? Are you finally going pro as a PI?'

'Err... not officially. But this one's different. The caller's a friend of my teacher. My teacher even texted me, urging me to help.'

'Alright, brief me. Don't forget, I'm your loyal sidekick.'

Vik smirked. 'Fair enough. The client is an elderly gentleman, Atul Mitra. Retired government officer. Yesterday, he lost his eyesight in what appears to be a freak accident, though he suspects foul play. The police are baffled. His son Pratul is coming over to discuss the matter. Let's see if there's something I can do.'

Pratul Mitra arrived an hour later. He was a man in his late twenties, standing about five foot nine with a fair complexion. A neatly trimmed beard and moustache framed his face. He wore a half-sleeve sky-blue shirt paired with dark denim, and his black-framed spectacles gave him a sharp, studious look. I welcomed him into the living room.

After a brief exchange of pleasantries, Vik leaned forward, clasping his hands. 'Alright, Pratul. Start from the beginning. Let's talk about your family first.'

Pratul's voice was low and raspy, punctuated by frequent coughs—a clear sign of the bad cold he was battling.

'We're based in Delhi. I was born and raised there. Dad retired from government service about a year ago. Around the same time, I lost my mom. Our ancestral home is in Agarpara, a serene suburb near the Ganges. It's where my late grandfather lived. After Mom's passing, Dad decided to move there. I've been in the UK, studying and working, but Dad wanted me back. I returned to Delhi last month but haven't joined a new job yet. That's our story.'

Vik nodded, his gaze steady. 'Alright. What exactly happened yesterday?'

'It was around 2 pm. Someone knocked on the front door. Dad opened it but found no one there. Then, he heard a whistle, and out of nowhere, some liquid splashed into his eyes. He said it burned terribly, and he lost his sight almost instantly.'

'A liquid?' Vik asked, eyebrows raised.

'Yes. We've no idea where it came from. Dad didn't see anyone.'

'What did the doctor say? Was it acid?'

'The doctor was clueless. He said the cornea in both eyes is severely damaged. Only a transplant can fix it. He believes it was some unknown chemical. The police haven't found any leads either.'

'And no one else was home at the time?'

'That's another puzzle. Our old servant, Sundar, who's been with us since my grandfather's time, went missing after the incident.'

At that moment, our maid entered, balancing a tray of tea and snacks. The rich aroma of freshly brewed tea filled the room.

'Please, have something,' Vik offered. 'You must be exhausted. I'm guessing you came straight here after seeing your father?'

Pratul's head snapped up, his expression startled, 'How did you…?'

Vik gestured towards Pratul's shirt pocket, 'Your train ticket. It's peeking out.'

Sure enough, the corner of a printed e-ticket protruded, the Indian Railways logo unmistakable.

'May I?' Vik asked, extending his hand.

Pratul hesitated but eventually handed over the ticket. Vik studied it briefly before handing it back. 'You arrived in Kolkata just a couple of hours ago.'

'Yes. I was already on the train when Dad called me about the incident,' Pratul admitted. 'But I had another reason to visit.'

'And that is?'

'We plan to sell all our Kolkata properties to fund a new business. The Agarpara house is old but spacious. We've already found a buyer—a promoter named Sujit Singhania. I was here to assist Dad with the paperwork, but now… everything's changed. I'm planning to take him to Delhi for treatment. Honestly, I'm not sure how you can help. The police are already investigating. I came because Dad insisted.'

Vik nodded, his expression thoughtful, 'I'm not a professional detective, but I've assisted the police several times. Since your father's friend requested, I'll look into it. Let's start with a small detail—who called the doctor?'

'Our neighbour, Mr Bimal Sen. He's been a pillar of support. He even sent his part-time servant to help out today.'

'Tell me about your grandfather,' Vik said, his tone shifting to one of curiosity.

'He worked for the Archaeological Survey of India. A man of adventure, he travelled extensively and penned several acclaimed travelogues. Most of his earnings went into the Agarpara house.'

'His name?'

'Rudra Prasad Mitra.'

A faint smile crossed Vik's face. 'Ah, I've read some of his work. He had a way with words.'

'He passed away five years ago.'

Vik leaned back, tapping his fingers on the armrest, 'That should do for now. I'll visit the house this afternoon. Share the address and your mobile number.'

Once Pratul had left, Vik turned to me, 'What's your take, Rik?'

I shrugged, 'It's bizarre. But don't you think you should've asked more questions? How do you plan to work with so little information?'

Vik's lips curled into a knowing smile, 'Sometimes, Rik, it's better to see than to hear.'

***

We reached Agarpara at around 4:00 pm. Atul Mitra's house was far from the city centre, perched gracefully along the Ganges Riverbanks. A high boundary wall enclosed the premises, within which sprawled a sizeable garden. The view from the garden—overlooking the tranquil river—was breathtaking. A paved pathway sliced through the greenery, stretching from the main gate to the house's front door. The house itself, an old two-storied structure, stood with quiet dignity. Each floor housed four spacious rooms, their aged walls echoing stories of the past.

Pratul greeted us at the entrance. 'Come in,' he said, his voice tinged with weariness. We followed him into the living room on the ground floor.

'Let me call Dad,' he said. 'He's quite shaken, as you can imagine.'

Five minutes later, Pratul returned, guiding an elderly gentleman. Atul Mitra appeared to be in his sixties, dressed in a white kurta-pyjama that added to his stately presence. Despite his stout build, the bandages over his eyes and the stick he gripped hinted at vulnerability. His grey hair and clean-shaven face were markers of age, yet his posture suggested a man who had once stood tall and resolute.

After a round of introductions, Mr. Mitra said, 'My friend spoke highly of you. Thank you for coming. I'm sorry to impose, but the police… they're not making much progress.'

Vik leaned forward, his tone reassuring. 'We've heard about the incident from your son, but I'd like to hear it from you in your own words. Could you tell me what happened in detail?'

Mr. Mitra sighed, his voice heavy with frustration, 'Yesterday, after lunch, my servant Sundar mentioned he had some work in the garden and stepped out. I decided to rest for a while. I was woken by a knock on the front door. I called out for Sundar several times, but he didn't respond. So, I went to open the door myself. No one was there—or at least, I didn't see anyone. Just as I stepped forward to look better, a sharp whistling sound came from my left. Then, out of nowhere, something warm splashed into my eyes. It burned… it burned like hell. The pain was unbearable. I must have cried out before collapsing. I don't know how long I lay there. I only woke up when my neighbour, Mr Sen, found me. And that's when I realized… I couldn't see anymore.'

His voice faltered, the weight of his words sinking into the room.

'What about Sundar?' Vik asked gently.

'I don't know,' Mr. Mitra replied. 'He's been missing ever since he went to the garden.'

'How long has he been working here?'

'Sundar was with my father during the last five years of his life. After that, he stayed, looking after the house when I wasn't around. I used to visit twice a year before my retirement.'

'Why didn't you sell the house earlier instead of depending on a servant?' Vik inquired.

A faint smile crossed Mr. Mitra's face. 'This house holds my childhood memories. I was too attached to part with it. But now, with Pratul back and needing funds for his new business, I've decided to sell it and return to Delhi.'

'Do you own any other property in Kolkata?'

'Not really,' Mr. Mitra replied. 'Just a few pieces of my mother's jewellery kept in our joint locker at the bank. I'll withdraw those tomorrow as well. The doctor says I might regain my sight after the transplant. Pratul wants to take me to Delhi soon for the treatment. The house deal should also be finalized by tomorrow.'

Vik leaned back slightly in his chair, his fingers drumming lazily on the armrest as he spoke. 'Your father was a government servant and a globetrotter, I hear. He must have done well for himself. This house is certainly a testament to that.'

'He was involved in several ventures besides his job. But he spent most of his money on travel and this house. He didn't leave much for us apart from this property.'

'Even so, the house looks splendid. Everything here seems top-notch,' Vik observed.

Mr. Mitra nodded, 'True. The promoter is buying it fully furnished. We managed to strike a good deal.'

'Alright. You should rest now. I want to take a look around the house. Did your father have a study or a personal space where he kept his belongings?'

'Yes, on the first floor,' Mr. Mitra replied. 'But there's nothing valuable there—just books, half-finished manuscripts, diaries... all mundane stuff. I've never been interested in such things. But you're welcome to check it out. Pratul will show you the way.'

***

The study room on the first floor was impressively well-organized and likely maintained by Sundar. The shelves were packed with books on various subjects, while a separate rack held manuscripts and diaries. A sturdy table with a chair and a classic table lamp stood at the centre. The room also featured sculptures and idols scattered artfully around, along with a few oil paintings adorning the walls.

Vik's eyes lingered on a painting of a young man sporting a beard and moustache, dressed regally in a turban and elaborate jewellery.

'This is Maharaja Bhupinder Singh of Patiala,' Vik remarked, his tone reflective. 'He's wearing the legendary Patiala necklace. If I recall correctly, it was crafted with over 3,000 diamonds and numerous Burmese rubies. Tragically, the necklace was lost—most likely stolen. Years later, the central diamond, the De Beers diamond, appeared in a Geneva auction. Its buyer remains a mystery. Eventually, part of the necklace was recovered in a jewellery shop.

The original manufacturer restored it, substituting the missing diamonds with synthetics and creating a replica of the De Beers diamond. But the majority of the original jewels remain missing.'

'Sounds fascinating. Do you think this painting is valuable?' Pratul asked, his curiosity piqued.

Vik gestured toward the signature in the bottom-right corner. 'Not in monetary terms. See this? Your grandfather painted it. All these artworks here are his creations. Not only was he a talented writer, but he was also a remarkable painter. Unfortunately, you never got to know him well.'

Pratul sighed, 'I barely had a chance. He was always travelling. During his final years, he stayed here, but he'd visit us in Delhi once a year, usually for a week. He'd always bring me gifts.'

'So, this is your first time here?' Vik asked.

Pratul shrugged, 'Yeah, I've never been to Kolkata before.'

Vik turned to me, 'Rik, look through the diaries and find me the latest entry. I'll examine the rest of the room.' He pointed toward the rack filled with manuscripts and diaries.

While I sifted through the diaries, Vik snapped a photo of Maharaja's painting with his smartphone before focusing on other objects in the room. After a few minutes, I found what I was looking for.

'Here,' I said, holding up a diary. 'The last entry is dated November 19, 2016. The page after that is missing, but the next page has faint impressions from pen pressure. We need a pencil.'

Vik grabbed a pencil from the table and rubbed it gently over the blank page. Slowly, words emerged:

Where can I hide all these treasures? I don't know how that guy learned about these gold coins. He will expect me to keep them in the house. I should bury them in the garden and build something over them so no one can find out.

'Gold coins?' I exclaimed, my voice rising.

Vik turned to Pratul, 'Did you know about this?'

Pratul shook his head, looking genuinely startled. 'Not at all.'

'We need to ask your father,' Vik said firmly.

Flipping through the diary, Vik frowned and ran his fingers over several pages. The lines on his forehead deepened as he concentrated. Finally, he handed the diary back to me.

I opened the diary again and rubbed my hand on the pages as Vik had done. I found nothing unusual. They were ordinary smooth pages, full of entries.

'Let's check your room before we go downstairs,' he said to Pratul.

Pratul's room was next to the study and just as immaculate.

Vik's gaze landed on a trolley bag near the corner. 'Looks like you haven't unpacked yet,' he observed.

'Yeah, I've been too busy. I'll get to it after you leave,' Pratul replied.

The clothes he had worn earlier were hanging neatly from the door hook. On the table lay his wallet and watch, along with a face shield and mask—lingering reminders of the pandemic, even though most people had been vaccinated by now. Judging by the trolley bag, much of his belongings were still packed. It had been a hectic day for him.

***

Atul Mitra seemed genuinely baffled when Vik asked about hidden gold coins.

'All that he left for us is this old house and a few ornaments in the bank,' Atul said, shaking his head. 'Not more than a commoner leaves for his heir. It must be some kind of bad joke if he wrote about gold coins.'

Vik, unfazed, requested to inspect the garden.

Pratul, visibly fatigued, said, 'If you'll excuse me, I'm dead tired. Our servant Hari will show you around the garden.'

'New servant?' Vik inquired.

'No,' Pratul clarified. 'He's Mr Sen's part-time servant. Our neighbour was kind enough to send him here to help out.'

'Ah, yes,' Vik said thoughtfully. 'I'd like to speak to Mr Sen as well.'

'I'll call him and let him know you're coming,' Pratul offered.

Dusk had already set in by the time we stepped into the garden. The fading sunlight cast long shadows across the grounds, lending an eerie beauty to the place. We walked to the spot on the left side of the front door where Atul claimed to have heard the strange whistling sound. Despite a thorough search, we found nothing of significance.

Vik's expression softened as he turned toward the river. The setting sun cast golden streaks over the water, its gentle ripples catching the light like scattered jewels. The warm hues of dusk painted the sky in soft amber and crimson, blending seamlessly with the river's calm. It was a rare, tranquil moment amid the mystery, offering a brief but welcome pause. We stood there in quiet appreciation for a while, letting the peaceful scene ease the day's tension.

Breaking the stillness, I ventured, 'I wonder if the gold coins are still buried in the garden. Sundar came here before he disappeared. What if he found the coins, took them, and fled?'

Vik glanced at me, his gaze steady, 'Speculation won't get us anywhere, Rik. We need to analyze this logically and keep a neutral perspective. Let's meet the neighbour now.'

***

Bimal Sen's house was modest in size. Unfortunately, I couldn't get a good look at it as night had already descended. The living room, though small, was tastefully decorated and filled with bookshelves, hinting at his fondness for reading.

Bimal Sen, an octogenarian, was a lean man with grey hair and deeply wrinkled skin. Dressed in a white kurta-pyjama, he exuded a kind and approachable demeanour.

Vik began, 'Sorry for disturbing you at this hour. Could you please tell us what happened to Mr Mitra yesterday? How did you find him?'

Bimal nodded slowly, 'After lunch, my wife went to the roof to fetch the laundry when she heard a scream. She was certain it came from Atul's house. At first, I didn't think much of it, but she insisted something was wrong. So, I went to check. What a dreadful sight it was. Atul was lying unconscious near the front door. His eyes… they looked terrible—red and watery. His servant was nowhere to be seen. I immediately called a doctor and sent my servant to help. Later, I learned he'd lost his eyesight. Such a tragedy.'

'Did you see anyone else nearby?' Vik pressed.

'No,' Bimal replied, 'The house was deserted.'

'Was the main gate leading to the garden open?'

'Yes. Atul usually keeps it unlocked during the day since there's no security guard. His servant locks it at night.'

'Did you know Mr Rudra Prasad Mitra?' Vik asked, shifting the conversation.

A warm smile spread across Bimal's face, 'Oh, yes. Rudra and I were close friends. Every morning, we'd have tea together in his garden, enjoying the view of the Ganga. What a remarkable man he was!'

'How do you feel about the house being sold?'

Bimal's smile faded, 'It's a shame—such a beautiful house. Rudra would never have sold it. But his son… he doesn't seem to care for it.'

'Have you met his grandson?'

'No,' Bimal said, shaking his head, 'This is his first visit here. To be honest, I haven't set foot in that house since Rudra passed away until yesterday. I don't know Atul very well. I'm just doing what any neighbour would do.'

***

As we stepped out of Bimal Sen's house, the faint glow of a streetlamp illuminated the quiet lane between the two properties. Shadows shifted lazily under the dim light, and the stillness of the evening settled around us.

Vik pulled out his cell phone and made a brief call. 'We're here, Pratip,' was all he said.

In the distance, a motorbike roared to life and approached us, coming to a halt near the houses. The bike bore the markings of a well-known food delivery service, and the rider was dressed in the company's uniform. The young man, slim with a dark complexion, had earphones trailing to a phone in his pocket.

Vik greeted him with a nod. 'Sorry to bother you like this, friend. I'll make it worth your while.'

Pratip waved it off with a faint smile. 'It's no problem. I've got a few days off, and some extra cash is always welcome.'

'Good,' Vik said, his tone crisp. 'I need you to monitor these two houses. Keep track of everyone entering or leaving except the police. If anyone leaves, follow them and let me know where they go.'

Pratip gave a firm nod, 'You can count on me.'

Vik handed him some cash, which Pratip tucked into his

pocket before revving up his bike and disappearing into the night.

As we walked toward our car, Vik broke the silence, 'He was a classmate of mine. He lost his father a few years ago and has been struggling ever since. Poor guy.'

I glanced back at the lane, now cloaked in the streetlamp's feeble light, as the faint hum of Pratip's bike faded into the distance.

***

Vik's phone rang just as we reached the highway. He tapped the screen, connecting the call to the car's speaker system.

'Hello,' he said.

A hoarse voice responded, 'Can I talk to Victor Chatterjee?'

'Yes, speaking.'

'My name is Sujit Singhania. I understand you visited a house today that I'm very interested in.'

'Looks like you're well-informed,' Vik replied calmly.

'I am. I've no issue with your visit,' Singhania said, his tone sharpening, 'What concerns me is what you've stirred up.'

'Can you elaborate?' Vik asked, his voice steady.

'I believe you've put the idea into the owner's head that hidden gold coins are buried in that house. His son called me a few minutes ago to say they're postponing the sale until they find those coins. That's a major problem for me.'

'It's their decision,' Vik said coolly, 'What can I do about it?'

Singhania's voice rose, a note of menace creeping in. 'Listen, Chatterjee. I don't know how much you know about me, but I'll tell you this—you don't want me as an enemy.'

Despite the car's air conditioning, I felt a bead of sweat trickle down my temple.

Vik's tone turned icy, 'Same here, Singhania.'

A tense silence followed before the line went dead.

Moments later, Vik's phone buzzed with a message notification. He glanced at the screen briefly and handed the phone to me. It was a text from Pratul. It read:

Mr Chatterjee, we have decided to postpone the sale of the house until the gold coins are found. Dad wasn't interested, but I've convinced him. If Grandpa left something for us, it must be uncovered. Kindly assist us in finding the treasure while investigating the attack on Dad.

I leaned back in my seat, the weight of the message sinking in. The speed at which events were unravelling left me disoriented, a flurry of questions swirling in my mind as the car sped down the highway.

***

After dinner, Vik settled on the sofa, idly scrolling through his phone. I sat across from him, waiting for him to share insights about the case. My curiosity was burning.

He finally spoke, 'Do you know which police officer is handling this investigation?'

'No,' I replied, intrigued.

'Avay. He texted me earlier and helped me with something I needed.'

'What kind of help?'

'I asked him for a list. Something the police could easily access but would've been tough for me to obtain.'

'What list?'

Vik gave me a pointed look, 'You should've figured it out by now.'

'I have no idea,' I admitted. 'Anyway, what does Avay think about the case?'

'He's suspicious of Singhania. Says the guy doesn't have a clean record and is linked to several goons.'

'Interesting. But how could they have done it? There was no one there when Mr Mitra opened the door. Although… I have some theories.'

Vik leaned forward, intrigued, 'Let's hear them.'

'They could've used a drone,' I suggested. 'I've seen it in movies. Drones can attack people, shoot bullets, or drop bombs. Maybe someone modified one to spray chemicals.'

Vik raised an eyebrow, 'Creative, but a bit far-fetched. Even if Singhania has money, such technology is mostly military-grade. Think simpler.'

'Alright,' I said, scratching my head. 'What if it wasn't an attack? Maybe a poisonous insect stung him by accident.'

'That's more plausible,' Vik admitted, 'But I doubt such an insect exists here. This isn't the Amazon rainforest.'

'Then what do you think happened?'

Vik's gaze turned thoughtful, 'I have some ideas, but I must research them before sharing. Meanwhile, I have something interesting to show you.'

He unlocked his phone and opened a photo of the painting of Maharaja Bhupinder Singh wearing the Patiala necklace.

'Look at the necklace,' Vik said. 'How many chains do you see?'

'Four,' I counted.

'Now check the original necklace online. Tell me how many chains it has.'

I took his phone and searched. The original Patiala necklace had five chains.

'What do you make of that?' Vik asked.

'Maybe Rudra Prasad made a mistake while painting it?' I offered.

'Did he?' Vik smirked. 'Look at the central diamond. Does it match the original?'

I inspected the image closely. 'No, it's yellow in the painting. It looks like a topaz.'

'Exactly. It's not a diamond at all. Do you think it's just an artistic whim?'

I hesitated. 'What are you suggesting? That Rudra Prasad somehow copied the necklace?'

Vik's eyes narrowed. 'Possibly. In one of his travelogues I read earlier, he mentioned being at the Geneva auction where the De Beers diamond was sold. He even tried to buy it but couldn't. There's no mention of him acquiring other parts of the necklace, but we might find clues in his diaries or manuscripts.'

'And the gold coins? Pratul wants you to find those, too.'

Vik leaned back, blowing a raspberry, 'I have no idea.'

Later, I took my tablet to bed, scrolling through the social media profiles of everyone we'd encountered so far. I knew Vik had already done this—he always did when working on a case—but I couldn't resist.

Pratul's accounts were private, meaning that only friends could access them. I couldn't see anything other than his profile picture, which showed him standing at the edge of a cliff in an epic style, facing backwards with both hands stretched. Atul Mitra and Bimal Sen didn't have social media accounts, which wasn't surprising for their age group.

Sujit Singhania's profile, however, was wide open. His photos showcased a life of luxury: expensive clothes, high-end watches, and extravagant trips worldwide, particularly to the Middle East.

One glance was enough to confirm he wasn't someone to mess with.

Feeling restless, I shifted gears and searched for Chris Robinson, the Serpent Man. His profile picture featured him holding a massive snake, gently patting its head. It was bizarrely mesmerising, but I quickly closed the app, unsure what the next day might bring.

***

Vik decided to take the day off work, suspecting something significant might happen in the morning.

Around 10 am, his phone buzzed. He answered it quickly.

'What's up, Pratip?' Vik asked.

I couldn't hear what Pratip said on the other end, but Vik's expression remained calm.

'Okay, stay on them,' Vik replied before hanging up.

'Pratip is doing a great job,' he declared.

'What did he inform you now?' I asked, my curiosity piqued.

'Both the father and son have gone to the bank. Only Mr Sen's part-time servant is at the house.'

'Yes, Mr Mitra mentioned he would visit the bank today. But doesn't that mean the house is unguarded? Anyone searching for gold coins could easily break in now. I hope your friend is keeping an eye on the house. If Singhania sends someone…'

Vik interrupted me. 'No, Pratip is outside the bank.'

'Oh. Then shouldn't we go to the house now? Otherwise, we might lose the coins.'

'Wait, Rik. Not so fast. Avay is coming in a while. He texted me. We'll head out after that.'

I couldn't hide my frustration at Vik's calm demeanour. Why

was he allowing Singhania a free pass to search the house? That part-time servant wouldn't stand a chance if someone tried to break in—and could probably be bribed anyway.

A quarter of an hour passed, and Pratip called again to inform us that the father and son were returning home. Too late, perhaps, I thought grimly.

Just then, the doorbell rang.

'Must be your friend, Avay,' I said, walking toward the door. As I reached for the doorknob, a faint hissing sound stopped me in my tracks.

'Stop,' Vik shouted, springing up from the sofa. He lunged toward me, grabbing my T-shirt and pulling me back.

'Wait here. Don't open the door,' he whispered urgently before rushing to his bedroom.

I stood frozen, bewildered. Moments later, Vik returned wearing a face shield.

'Why are you wearing that? What's outside?' I asked, still in shock.

'Terror is waiting behind this door, Rik. Stay back,' he said, urgency sharp in his muffled voice as his eyes flicked toward the door, making my stomach churn.

Vik opened the door cautiously. I stood rooted to the spot, horrified by what lay outside.

It was a reddish-black snake, about a meter long, its hood spread wide in a menacing display. The instant the door opened, a low-pitched whistling sound cut through the air. At that precise moment, the snake did the most unexpected thing—it hissed sharply and spat a stream of liquid, aiming directly at Vik's eyes. Thankfully, his face shield protected him.

Without a moment's hesitation, Vik seized the snake by its neck, swiftly transferring it into our laundry basket. He flipped the basket upside down, trapping the writhing creature inside. My mind raced with a single question: Strange! How did he know? How does he always know?

'Don't come within two meters of this basket, Rik,' Vik warned. 'It can still spit venom through the holes.' He placed a heavy book on top of the basket for good measure.

'What kind of snake is this? Where did it come from?' I asked, my voice shaky.

'This is a spitting cobra, Rik. This is the same snake that attacked and blinded Mr Mitra.'

At that moment, Inspector Avay burst into the room, his face flushed and eyes wide with astonishment. 'Who was that man?' he blurted out, his voice tinged with amazement. 'He just bumped into me while running out of your house. It happened so quickly; I couldn't catch him.'

Vik took out his phone, held it to Avay, and asked, 'This man?'

Avay's eyes widened. 'Yes. But…'

'No time for chatter, Avay,' Vik said, cutting him off. 'Let's move. And stay away from the basket. We'll deal with it later.' Avay glanced at the basket, his eyes widening further, but nodded quickly.

'Alright, let's go,' he could only say.

***

As we climbed into Avay's police car, Vik asked, 'Where is your backup?'

'Our sub-inspector is already headed towards Agarpara with three constables. How many people are we up against?'

'At least three or four.'

'My God. Is this a gang?'

'Not a gang, but they're local hires.'

'Oh, I see. But why did you ask for that list yesterday? How is that connected?'

'Did you go through it?'

'No. Didn't get time.'

'You wouldn't have to ask if you had. Anyway, let's hope we get there in time.'

As we sped along the highway, Vik's phone rang.

'Yes, Pratip. What's the update? Going out? Okay, don't lose him. Send me the GPS location once he reaches his destination, and please, don't blow your cover. We're on the way,' he disconnected the call.

The car lapsed into silence for a while. Finally, as we neared Agarpara, Vik's phone buzzed with a message notification.

'GPS location received from Pratip,' he said. 'Move ahead. We're heading to Titagarh. Send this location to your sub-inspector. We don't have much time.'

Titagarh, an industrial area two railway stations beyond Agarpara, had a grimy, congested look. It took us fifteen minutes to reach the location, a bustling market area near the highway.

We spotted Pratip waiting on his bike, parked across the street. He pointed to a red two-storied building one block ahead. Moments later, the other police car arrived and parked behind us.

'Go in. Weapons ready,' Avay commanded.

We moved in first, followed by the constables. The building's ground floor housed a grocery shop, where a fat, dark-complexioned man sat behind the counter. A constable restrained him before he could raise an alarm. We took the stairs to the first floor, where a dimly lit corridor led to three evenly spaced doors. Faint voices came from behind the first door.

Vik kicked it open, and we barged in. It was a small room, sparsely furnished with a table, a chair, and a single bed.

What I saw left me stunned. Standing before me were Pratul and an unexpected figure: Chris Robinson, the serpent man. Both looked packed and ready to flee.

Chris reacted first, swinging a punch at Vik, who blocked it and retaliated with a swift uppercut, knocking him out. Pratul froze, his face draining of colour as Avay aimed a gun at him.

In one corner of the room lay a young man, bound with duct tape at his wrists and ankles, his mouth gagged. It didn't take long to realize the truth: Pratul and Chris were not just acquainted; they had been holding this man captive.

I turned to Vik, overwhelmed. 'What's going on here? Why is Chris Robinson here? Who is this man? And Pratul, how is he involved?'

Vik's voice was calm but firm, 'This is not Pratul. He's an impostor. His real name is Ajay Gupta. That's the real Pratul,' he said, pointing to the bound man on the floor.

My jaw dropped, 'What?'

Avay's bewilderment matched mine, 'What the hell is going on?' he demanded.

'I'll explain later,' Vik replied tersely. 'For now, arrest these two. The shopkeeper downstairs is likely involved as well. Search the other rooms; you'll find the servant Sundar in one of them.'

I finally found my voice. 'What a deadly plan! But why all this?'

Vik's gaze bore into Ajay as he asked, 'Where is it, Ajay? Give it to me.'

Ajay hesitated before glancing at the table where a handbag lay. Vik grabbed it, unzipped it, and pulled out a necklace. The craftsmanship was exquisite, and the design matched the one in Rudra Prasad's painting.

'This is what it was all about,' Vik said, holding up the

necklace. 'The remnant of the famous Patiala necklace, crafted from original diamonds and Burmese rubies. Lost to history… until now.'

***

'Impersonation is difficult in this age of social media but not impossible. Ajay and Chris have proven that, though it did not end well for them,' Vik said while sipping tea.

'He showed me a fake passport and ID,' Avay grunted.

'Fake documents can be forged overnight these days. Forgeries and counterfeits are a thriving business in every city,' Vik chuckled.

It was early afternoon. We were sitting in Atul Mitra's garden, enjoying tea and snacks. The setting sun reflected in the river, creating a pleasant atmosphere. We were accompanied by Mr Mitra, Pratul (the real one), and Inspector Avay. Sundar had been rescued from the same house. Both Pratul and Sundar had received first aid and were now feeling better.

'I can tell you the entire story, but let's hear it from the man who experienced it,' Vik said, looking at Pratul.

Pratul's height and physique were almost identical to Ajay's, although he was fairer and more handsome. Now, cleaned up and shaved, he looked even better despite the visible injuries on his face and hands. He had been beaten badly.

Pratul leaned back, his face etched with both exhaustion and relief, 'I can't believe I'm free. Those three days felt like a lifetime,' he murmured, his voice trembling. Vik gave him a reassuring nod. 'You've been through a lot, but now we need to piece everything together.'

In a weak but steady voice, Pratul began, 'Grandpa sent me a letter a month before he died while I was in England. He mentioned in that letter that he had found and purchased all the missing parts of the famous Patiala necklace and had it reassembled. He spent a fortune on it. He didn't tell Dad because he thought Dad would sell it. Grandpa instructed me to keep it in the family. Dad was also keen to sell the house and start a business, but Grandpa was dead against it.'

'This is contrary to the impression you gave us yesterday, Mr Mitra,' Vik interrupted. 'You said you were emotionally attached to this house. It now seems you couldn't sell it earlier because of your son. He might not have agreed.'

Atul Mitra remained silent.

Pratul continued, 'That's true. I had planned to renovate this house and convert it into a tourist spot, showcasing its historical charm and the legacy of my grandfather's work. After Mom passed away, Dad started living here. But soon, loneliness engulfed him, making him depressed. My job in London wasn't going well, so I decided to come back and stay with Dad. That's why we agreed to sell the house, return to Delhi, and start a business. Ajay was my flatmate in London and also my best friend.'

'You told him about the necklace?' Avay asked.

'Yes. That was so stupid of me. I trusted him blindly. I even showed him the letter. It was mentioned in the letter that the necklace was kept in the bank locker along with other jewellery,' Pratul sighed.

'Okay, carry on,' Vik said.

'Dad went to Delhi to pick me up at the airport. He was so delighted to see me. After staying with me for a week, he returned to Agarpara to finish packing and dispose of small items before selling the house. I wanted to accompany him, but Dad insisted I rest and enjoy myself. So, I spent the month catching up with old friends in Delhi. I was supposed to visit Kolkata yesterday before the house's final sale. I had also planned to take the Patiala necklace from the bank to Delhi but didn't mention it to Dad. A week before, Ajay called me. I was delighted to know he had come to Delhi. I met him at his hotel, where he introduced me to Chris Robinson as his friend. I was intrigued to find that Chris was a snake expert travelling in India for a couple of months. I told Ajay I was planning to visit Kolkata to sell our properties. Ajay called me the next day and said Chris wanted to visit Kolkata before returning to the US. Both Ajay and Chris decided to accompany me. But the problem was that Chris's return ticket was for today. He wanted to visit Kolkata earlier. That day, we met again. Ajay purchased urgent Tatkal tickets for all three of us on the Rajdhani Express two days earlier than my original date. Ajay suggested I surprise Dad by not informing him about my early arrival. I fell for it. It was also my first visit to Kolkata. I was so excited that I couldn't see through their plan. Ajay asked me about our family and our house in Agarpara, and I told him everything like a fool. Although he already knew a lot about us, being my best friend. Ajay told me he has contacts in Kolkata and would arrange a car for us.

'When we reached Kolkata and got into the car Ajay had arranged, they took me captive. They confiscated my belongings and phone, leaving me in that house in Titagarh. They tortured me for my social media passwords. The shopkeeper brought me food, and there was no chance to escape. Chris occasionally visited but never spoke to me. I didn't see Ajay again until this morning. By then, they had already secured the necklace and planned to escape to Dubai when you caught them.'

Everyone remained silent.

Finally, Vik spoke, 'I hope you can understand how dangerous their plan was. Letting Pratul and Mr Mitra withdraw the necklace from the bank and trying to steal it later could have been a choice. But there was uncertainty in that. Ajay had all the information to impersonate Pratul. The problem was his father, the only person who could at once recognize the impostor. So, he had to be taken care of. But killing Mr Mitra would not help as his signature was needed to open the bank locker. So, Chris and Ajay planned to blind Mr Mitra, the only person who could recognize the original Pratul in this city. Another potential problem was Sundar. He had been in this house for a long time. Though he had never met Pratul, he could have seen his picture. So, the duo didn't take any chance and abducted Sundar on that day when he was busy working in the garden. I am quite sure that they had kept an eye on this house from the day they had arrived, including entry and exits, the right time to attack, the routine of the inhabitants, and all that stuff. They found out that this neighbourhood stays quiet past midday. The main gate to the garden also remains unlocked during the daytime.'

Vik stopped to gather his thoughts and started, 'Now Chris is a snake charmer. He had a red spitting cobra with him. I am not sure how he got hold of it. They are found in Asia and Africa, with some species in India. Probably, he collected one while travelling in India. Moreover, he performs snake shows all over the world. He must have a special cargo and permission to carry his snakes. Perhaps he brought this snake to Kolkata in some special container that Pratul was unaware of. Cargo is usually not checked on the train as thoroughly as in a flight due to less stringent security protocols. Being an adept snake charmer, Chris had trained this cobra to spit venom at the blow of a specially designed whistle, producing a low-pitched sound. Many studies say that snakes cannot hear as such, but they perceive low-pitched sounds as vibrations and can respond to them. After abducting Sundar, Chris knocked on the door, placed the snake in front of it and waited at a distance. We usually look ahead when we open the door, not at the floor. So, Mr Mitra could not see the snake. Chris made the snake attack him by blowing the whistle while keeping himself hidden. As Mr Mitra was writhing in pain, Chris took the snake and escaped. Their work was done for that day. Sundar was imprisoned in the same house where they kept Pratul.'

Avay shook his head. 'A professional snake charmer turned criminal mastermind. Desperation can truly make anyone dangerous.'

Vik nodded, 'If you grasp the sheer value of the Patiala necklace, you'd understand why he risked everything to turn to crime. For him, the potential reward outweighed the danger.'

He paused briefly before continuing, 'Now, where were we? Ah yes, the next day, as planned, Ajay arrived impersonating Pratul. He had access to all of Pratul's social media profiles through his phone and made sure that his face was not seen on any social media platform by making all profiles private. His friends could still see his pictures, but Ajay knew he had no friends in this city. So being Pratul for one day was not difficult anymore. Of course, he had other things to take care of as he knew the police would be visiting the house. He had bought another e-ticket in Pratul's name, with the day before yesterday being the date of the journey. Ajay knew Pratul's mannerisms very well. He only had to fake a common cold to talk in a hoarse voice. Everything was set. But Mr Mitra created another problem for him. Guess what?'

Vik stopped.

'He called you,' I said, the realization dawning on me as everything started to fall into place.

'Correct. Not only did he call me, but he also made Ajay visit me on the same day he had appeared. Ajay came to me reluctantly. He was prepared, although. He played Pratul's role nicely in front of me. He even kept the e-ticket in his pocket in such a way as to draw my attention. The problem with train e-tickets is that they are not stamped as boarding passes on a flight. So, there is no way of verifying whether you have travelled just by looking at it. Ajay felt that this was not enough to divert me from the track. After returning, he made a fake entry in Rudra Prasad's diary, mentioning gold coins, and tore the page so as not to be too obvious. He would have shown it to me if we hadn't found it ourselves. He didn't like that I took an interest in the painting of the Maharaja wearing a Patiala necklace and took a snap of it. He tactfully let Sujit Singhania loose on me by postponing the sale of the house. Even then, he was not sure whether he would succeed. That's why Ajay went to the bank today with Mr Mitra to withdraw the jewellery while Chris came to my house to launch another attack of the spitting cobra. He must have kept a watch on my house since yesterday and noticed no one else in the house apart from the two of us. He knew that if he could get any of us, I would be unable to stop them for the time being. And I think they would have escaped the country today.'

Avay said, 'True. I found two tickets to Dubai in their personal belongings.'

'How did you crack this ingenious plan?' I asked.

'The motive was obvious from the beginning. Someone wanted Mr Mitra not to see something. The next day of the incident, his son came to the house that no one in this city had seen. And now even the father couldn't see his son's face. I didn't see any family photos in this house. Even if there was one, Ajay might have hidden it before I visited the house.'

Mr Mitra said, 'There was a picture on the bookshelf in the living room.'

Vik continued, 'Then, all his social media profiles were locked so no one could see his face. He didn't know that his grandpa was a painter. All this seemed too much of a coincidence. But then he made the blunder of trying to put me off track with the forged diary entry about hidden gold coins in the garden.'

I interjected, 'Wait a second, Vik. How did you realize the diary entry was forged?'

Vik held up the diary, which had been brought at his request. 'Look here. The pressure of the handwriting on this page is much heavier than the rest of the diary. Rudra Prasad was an experienced writer—his handwriting would have been consistent. This discrepancy caught my attention.'

'But why tear the page and leave an imprint?' I asked, frowning.

'Ajay was clever. He knew an obvious entry about gold coins might seem suspicious as I would ask why no one had noticed it before. So, he wrote it with heavy pressure, leaving an imprint on the next page, and tore it off. Now, the entry was less conspicuous and could easily be missed. Ajay thought he had outwitted me. But that same trick gave him away. The rest of the diary pages were smooth and written with normal pressure. A perfect forgery wasn't enough to fool Victor Chatterjee. Overall, I concluded that this man deliberately tried to hinder the investigation. He aimed to divert my attention to something non-existent by mentioning gold coins. But why would he do that? Clearly, he was after something else—something he didn't want me to discover. If you had a bank locker and gold coins, would you ever keep them in the garden or the house? Only a fool would. So, I perceived that there was something in the bank locker that this man wanted, and he was also an impostor.

'The attack happened on the previous day. I understood that he had come to Kolkata at least one day earlier. So, I asked Avay to collect the passenger list of Rajdhani Express for the past three days. I found three first-class passengers travelling together in one coup - Pratul Mitra, Ajay Gupta and Chris Robinson. Now thanks to

Rik, I had some idea of who Chris was. I remembered the whistle that Mr Mitra had heard during the attack. I suspected that a snake had been used. A little internet search revealed everything I needed about the spitting cobra. I understood that Chris was hiding somewhere nearby and holding the real Pratul captive. I knew that at some point, Ajay would be visiting there. I planted my friend Pratip in front of the house. And he did a nice job.'

'What happened to the snake?' Pratul asked.

'Staff from the Alipore Zoo came and took it. They told me it would be a nice addition to their reptile house.'

'What will happen to the necklace?' I asked.

Avay said, 'Rudra Prasad Mitra bought all the missing parts from various places. He kept purchase proofs in the locker. So, Atul Mitra is the present owner of the necklace. He will decide what to do.'

'My dad's last wish was to keep it in the family. I intend to do the same,' Mr Mitra responded.

Vik said, 'I have a suggestion, Mr Mitra. I believe the company that manufactured the original Patiala necklace will buy it at its deserved price, as they had announced earlier. And that will be millions of dollars, more than enough to set up Pratul's business and to renovate this house into a heritage place. Of course, a dead man's wish is important, but I believe more important is the wish of the man who is still around.'

As I sat there, watching Vik calmly sip his tea after untangling such a complex web of lies and deceit, I could not help but marvel at his brilliance. His uncanny ability to see through chaos and uncover the truth left me in awe—something I could only hope to grasp, even while standing by his side.

The place felt serene in the dusk light, with a gentle breeze drifting from the river.

One Eye, One Shot

Barun Sen was not happy when he received a call from his maid at 3 pm.

'Sreelekha must be sleeping like a log again and not opening the door to the maid. This is the second time this month. I can't live in peace,' Barun mumbled to himself.

'Madam is not opening the door. What to do?'

'What can I do from the office? She will be awake in a while. I'll be home in an hour. Come back at 4 pm,' Barun replied, irritation creeping into his tone.

He finished his remaining work and left for home as soon as possible. Unfortunately, his mood did not improve as he encountered heavy traffic jams on the way.

It took him 45 minutes to reach his housing complex. By the time he arrived at the third floor, where his apartment was, he found the maid already standing there, her face a picture of unease.

'Madam is still not opening the door. I rang the bell several times,' she informed him nervously.

Barun frowned and pulled out his spare key to unlock the door.

'You're sleeping like the dead again, Sree,' Barun called out, frustration bubbling over as he stepped into the living room. But it was empty. Annoyed, he made his way to the bedroom.

What he saw inside horrified and shattered him. His legs buckled, and he collapsed to the floor. The maid let out a shrill cry and bolted down the hallway.

The sight was truly horrifying. Sreelekha lay lifeless on the bed, the curtains billowing in the breeze from an open window. An arrow jutted grotesquely from her left eye, transforming the serene room into a nightmarish tableau.

***

Inspector Arun Raut reached the housing complex Indrapuri. It was in a neighbourhood near Dumdum, known as the Garage. The complex was relatively old, consisting of several blocks, each with five floors. The murder had occurred on the third floor of block five. Raut found the security guard dozing at the entrance of the complex. He scolded him and headed for block five.

A constable ushered him to the bedroom where the victim was lying. Raut felt a chill creep up his spine as he examined the body. A black arrow had pierced her left eye, its shaft an unsettling detail against the stillness of her lifeless form. She was lying on the bed facing the window, her feet resting on the ground. It seemed likely she had been standing at the window when the arrow struck, sending her sprawling backwards onto the bed. Raut peered out the window and spotted a high-rise building under construction a few blocks away. The vantage point seemed ideal for the shot.

'What have you found?' he asked the constable.

'Nothing, sir. This is an old complex without CCTV. The security guard didn't see anyone entering or leaving, nor did any of the inhabitants,' the constable replied nervously.

'That's quite natural, isn't it?' Raut said, irritation evident. 'She was killed by an arrow—someone doesn't need to enter the complex to shoot an arrow. Tell me something useful.'

'Sir, the approximate time of the murder seems to be between 12 pm and 3 pm. The husband left for work at 8:30 am, and the maid left at noon. The victim was alive until then. The maid returned at 3 pm and found the door locked. We can confirm the time of death with the forensic team later.'

'Okay. You stay here. I'll enquire in the neighbourhood.'

Raut exited the complex and made his way toward the building under construction. The skeletal structure of the high-rise loomed ahead, its shadow stretching ominously over the neighbourhood. Raut's eyes darted to the windows and ledges, scanning for anything unusual. His mind was already piecing together possibilities.

The building was in its final phase of construction. A small room for a security guard stood at the entrance, its faded walls bearing the grime of neglect. Raut showed his badge and asked the guard, 'Did someone unusual visit the site today? Between 12 and 3 pm?'

The watchman, a man in his fifties, scratched his head thoughtfully. 'Actually, yes. A gentleman did come. There's an entry in the register. Check here.'

Raut leaned over the register, his eyes narrowing as he read the entry. The name 'M. Singh' was listed at 1:30 pm, along with a mobile number. Both the name and the number are probably fake, Raut mused, but he snapped a photo of the entry on his phone, nonetheless.

'Why do you say he was unusual?'

'Well, sir, first, he came at an odd time. Usually, people visit in the morning or late afternoon. You can see in the register that the last entry before him was at 11 am. Secondly, he looked unusual. He wore sunglasses the whole time. But when he took them off momentarily, I noticed he had a prosthetic eye and a scar on the same side of his face.'

'How old was he?'

'Looked to be in his forties, sir. Average height, dark-complexioned, but well-dressed in a suit. Looked like someone who could afford these flats.'

'Did he have any bags?'

'Yes, sir. A long sports bag. He said he was travelling and had come directly from the airport to visit the site.'

'What time did he leave? Why isn't the exit noted in the register?'

'Err... Sir,' the guard stammered, guilt evident in his expression, 'I went to take a leak. He must have left while I was away. I didn't see him leave.'

'Do you know where he went inside the building?'

'Probably to the site office, sir. It's on the ground floor of the last block. All the flats are still under construction, so there's nowhere else to go. You can check there. The site manager should be available.'

Raut reached the site office and met the manager, a tall, fair man with curly hair and rimless spectacles. Calmly, the manager stated that no one had visited him during the specified time, his composure only fuelling Raut's growing impatience to uncover the truth.

Raut pointed to a block that he thought would be the best vantage point for the murder and asked, 'Can I check this building? Do you have working elevators?'

'Yes, but the apartments are not yet handed over. So, no one stays here.'

'That makes them more prone to criminal activity, given your site's security status. You are sitting in an air-conditioned office and have no idea that one person entered at 1.30 pm. You are saying that he did not come to you. So, he could have gone anywhere. Now, come with me and show me this entire block.

We'll start from the top floor. I want to see only those apartments which are facing north.'

Raut and the manager began their search on the 17th floor. By the time they reached a north-facing bedroom on the 14th floor, Raut spotted a black cylinder-shaped plastic box lying on the floor. Its lid was ajar, and a black arrow peeked through it—identical to the one used in the murder.

Raut looked out the window, his gaze tracing the line of sight to the Indrapuri complex. The victim's bedroom window was unmistakable, and the view was disturbingly perfect.

The only thing that gnawed at Raut was the distance. It was over 200 meters. Can someone shoot an arrow with that much precision from this far? he wondered, his mind racing with possibilities.

***

Rajat Dutta, a young IPS officer, entered the Police Commissioner's office the following day. He was tall and stout, with a beard, moustache, and light brown eyes. The Commissioner, Hrishikesh Roy, had called him early in the morning and asked him to report immediately to his office. Rajat arrived as soon as he could, noting the heavy stillness in the air as he stepped inside.

'You seem worried, Sir,' Rajat observed, his tone laced with curiosity.

Commissioner Roy, a man in his fifties, was known for his composure. Despite his hair having turned completely grey, he still looked young and healthy. A faint beam of sunlight filtered through the blinds, catching the edge of his desk. He gestured for Rajat to sit and spoke thoughtfully.

'I want to give you a responsibility, Rajat. Don't fail me.'

'What is it, Sir?'

'Let me tell you a story first. It happened fifteen years ago. A young archer named Mohan Singh became a public hero, even after committing four murders with a bow and arrow.'

Rajat interrupted, 'I've read about this case, Sir. The one-eyed archer?'

'Yes, that's correct. I was the investigating officer on the case. Let me give you the details. Mohan Singh came from a low-income family but was exceptionally talented. Though his family originated from Punjab, he was born and raised here in Kolkata. His talent was discovered by a selector for the Indian Olympic team, who, by chance, attended a village fair where Mohan was hitting bullseyes across a large field using only a handmade wooden bow. Impressed, the selector arranged for Mohan to receive professional archery training. It soon became clear that Mohan was the greatest modern-day archer India had ever seen. He was selected to represent the country in the upcoming Olympics. Originally, a minister's son was supposed to be selected for the Games. However, he was moved to the reserve bench and replaced by Mohan. Only one selector protested, but the majority chose Mohan. The very next day, Mohan was attacked while returning home from practice. Two assailants stabbed him in the left eye. His life was saved, thanks to the timely arrival of the police, but he lost his left eye and received a deep cut on his left cheek. Despite Mohan's pleas that he only aimed with his right eye and that his performance would not be affected, the selectors were unconvinced. They reinstated the minister's son in his place.'

'That's a tragic story,' Rajat remarked, his voice tinged with sympathy.

'The real story begins here, Rajat. The day after the final selection, a murder occurred outside a liquor shop. A notorious political goon was shot in the left eye with an arrow and died on the spot. Later that day, a second murder occurred at a petrol pump. This victim was the first goon's assistant. The modus operandi was identical. When the police went to Mohan's house, he had already fled. While the search for him was underway, a third murder occurred three days later. This time, it was the selector who had opposed Mohan's selection. He was killed while sitting by a window in his home. The final and most daring murder sealed Mohan's fate. During an election campaign, the minister whose son replaced Mohan was shot similarly with an arrow from a building over 200 meters away. I was there. We pursued Mohan to a bridge, where he jumped into the river. Before he disappeared underwater, I was certain I had shot him. His body was never found. Days later, we received an anonymous tip that a body had been burned secretly in a crematorium near Mohan's village. Despite interrogating the villagers, including Mohan's parents, we found no confirmation. He was presumed dead in the police records. At least until yesterday,' Hrishikesh stopped, his eyes narrowing slightly.

'I heard about the murder yesterday,' Rajat said. 'Do you think it's the same man? Could it be someone copying his method?'

'That kind of accuracy from such a distance? No one else can achieve it—not even the Olympian gold medallist. It must be Mohan. Such talent is born once in a blue moon.'

'You want me to arrest him before he strikes again.'

'Yes, and as quickly as possible. Do you know why I'm worried? Those two goons Mohan killed were responsible for the attack on him. The minister and the selector orchestrated it. Our investigation later confirmed this. The goons were wanted for multiple murders, and the minister had connections to the underworld. The selector was complicit in several of the minister's crimes. There was never enough evidence to prosecute them. Mohan's actions turned him into a hero—a vigilante. The public rallied in his support. The city was in turmoil for days after his disappearance. Angry mobs burned a police car and assaulted officers. We had to use tear gas and batons to restore order. I don't want that chaos again. He must be behind bars—or in a body bag—before public sentiment shifts.'

'But he killed an innocent woman,' Rajat groaned. 'The people won't support him this time.'

'I wouldn't be so naive as to trust public opinion, Rajat,' Hrishikesh said with a bitter chuckle. 'You have no idea how easily tales can be twisted. Act fast. Time is running out.'

***

Rajat visited Indrapuri in the afternoon after reading Mohan Singh's files. Inspector Raut was already waiting for him and immediately began recounting everything he had discovered the day before.

Rajat interrupted, 'I've already read your report. Tell me what I don't know. How is the situation here? What are the reactions of the residents in this complex?'

'It's chaos. There are rumours spreading everywhere, Sir.'

'What kind of rumours?'

'The public is glorifying the killer. You're in plain clothes, Sir. Just take a stroll through the complex—you'll hear it yourself.'

Rajat nodded and moved ahead, his sharp gaze scanning the surroundings. The hum of hushed conversations and an occasional burst of laughter from children contrasted sharply with the tension in the air.

A crowd had gathered in a small park around the corner.

Rajat walked toward the group, blending in. The park, with its rusted swings and dry patches of grass, seemed to echo the unease among the people. An elderly woman noticed him and addressed him, 'Hey, son. Are you a newcomer?'

Rajat replied smoothly, 'Yes, I moved in just last week. I haven't had a chance to meet anyone yet.'

'Which block?'

'Err…what a terrible thing happened here yesterday,' Rajat said, hesitating. 'I don't know if it's safe to stay here anymore.'

'Nothing will happen to you, son, as long as you haven't done anything wrong. The one-eyed archer doesn't harm innocent people.'

'Really? Does that mean this lady did something wrong?' Rajat asked, feigning curiosity.

'Of course.' The woman lowered her voice conspiratorially. 'Haven't you heard? That gentleman, Barun, is her second husband. She told me once that her first husband died of a heart attack at only forty. Do you believe that story, son? Who was she trying to fool? I'm quite sure she poisoned her first husband. And,' she leaned closer, lowering her voice further, 'her character was quite questionable. Everyone calls a beautician to their home—my daughter-in-law does, too. But who calls a male beautician when their husband isn't around? Can you tell me that?'

Rajat had heard enough. His expression hardened as he said sternly, 'And how many people have you shared this story with?'

The woman recoiled, startled by the change in his tone. 'What is your name again, son? Which block are you living in?'

'Rajat Dutta, Assistant Commissioner of Police. I don't live here. And if you tell anyone else what you just told me, I'll have to arrest you for spreading rumours.'

The woman's face paled, and she stepped back in horror.

Rajat raised his voice, addressing the gathered crowd, 'Ladies and gentlemen, listen carefully. I'm with the Police, and I'm here to tell you that if I find anyone spreading rumours about the murder—especially glorifying the killer—I will arrest that person as an accomplice. Am I clear?'

The crowd fell silent, tension thick in the air. Even the children playing nearby paused, sensing the gravity of the moment.

As Rajat turned to leave, heading toward the exit gate, the elderly woman called after him, her voice now bolder, 'How many of us will you arrest, ACP? The whole city will say the same thing soon. Just wait and watch. The one-eyed archer is a messiah, and people will know it soon enough.'

Rajat paused, his jaw tightening at her audacity. He was about to respond when his phone rang, cutting him off.

The voice on the other end spoke urgently, 'Sir, you need to come to Sodepur immediately. There's been another murder by the one-eyed archer.'

***

Rajat reached the Sodepur Government Housing Complex as quickly as he could. It was a 60-year-old housing complex comprising about 60 old-fashioned, four-storied buildings. The sprawling campus housed roughly 450 apartments and around 1,000 inhabitants. Two large playgrounds lay within the complex, serving as its beating heart, where laughter and chatter often echoed through the evenings.

The murder had taken place in a block situated in front of one of the playgrounds. As Rajat approached, he noticed a field already teeming with a restless crowd. The murmurs and occasional exclamations carried a mix of fear and intrigue.

Inspector Avik Sarkar from the local police station stood nearby, his expression grim. He greeted Rajat with a wary look.

'Sir, the situation is getting out of control. We need to remove the body soon,' Avik said, his voice tight with urgency.

'Tell me what happened,' Rajat replied.

'A 35-year-old woman, Priyanka Sur, was murdered on the second floor of this block,' Avik said, pointing toward an isolated building on the southern edge of the playground. 'Her body was found on a bed in front of an open window, with a black arrow pierced in her left eye. That's the window.' He gestured emphatically toward it.

'Who else was in the apartment?'

'No one. She lived alone while her husband worked abroad.'

'Any sign of forced entry into the apartment?'

'Not at all. The door was locked from the inside. These are old buildings—no elevators, no CCTV. But the doors have in-built locks.'

'So, these doors can be locked from the outside by closing them with enough force?'

'Yes, of course. But we're fairly certain the arrow was shot from the rooftop of that building across the field.' Avik pointed to a block on the northern side of the playground.

'You found anything there?' Rajat asked, his curiosity sharpening.

'We got everything, Sir,' Avik said confidently. 'These rooftops are typically off-limits, accessible only to cable TV technicians. There's no direct staircase access. Each block has a ladder, usually chained and locked at the top floor corridor. The key is kept with the top-floor inhabitants. When a technician comes to repair the TV antennas, they ask for the key and return it after use.'

'Fascinating. Then?' Rajat remarked, arching an eyebrow.

'A middle-aged man asked for the ladder keys to that building a couple of hours ago, introducing himself as a cable TV technician. He was carrying a large bag. He returned the keys within 15 minutes. According to the top-floor inhabitant, he had a prosthetic eye and a scar on his face.' Avik's enthusiasm rose as he recounted the details.

'Did you check the rooftop?'

'Of course, Sir. Look what we found.'

Avik waved at a constable, 'Rana, bring what we found on the rooftop.'

The constable fetched a large transparent plastic bag from the police van. Inside were a black arrow and a cylinder-shaped arrow container.

'Well,' Rajat said, inspecting the evidence, 'What else?'

'If you want to look at the body, let's do it immediately. We must remove it soon, or the crowd will only grow larger. Already, rumours about the murder are spreading.'

'Do those rumours involve character assassinating the victim and glorifying the one-eyed archer as a punisher of evil people?' Rajat asked knowingly.

Avik's eyes widened, 'How did you know, Sir?'

Rajat sighed heavily, 'Let's go and check the body.'

***

The following day, Rajat found himself back in the Police Commissioner's office, his mood far worse than the day before. Hrishikesh had summoned him early in the morning to deliver news Rajat was unprepared for.

'The central Home Minister called this morning from New Delhi,' Hrishikesh began in a severe tone, sipping his coffee. 'He wants this case solved urgently. And he insists we take help from this guy—a professor of chemistry.'

'How ridiculous,' Rajat snapped, his frustration boiling over. 'Aren't we competent enough to solve the case? Why didn't you refuse, Sir?'

'That wasn't an option,' Hrishikesh replied, his tone measured. 'He said it's a matter of national security. The director of RAW personally recommended this man. According to them, the case hasn't been handled efficiently so far, and we're better off taking professional advice.'

'Unbelievable!' Rajat scoffed. 'Now the Kolkata Police has to follow the advice of a chemistry professor? And you agreed to this?'

'My hands are tied, my dear,' Hrishikesh said, his calm demeanour barely masking his own irritation. 'You'll work with this guy and solve the case. Otherwise, there'll be more trouble for the department. Already, social media is buzzing with memes and jokes about Mohan being a vigilante hero while defaming the victims. The situation could spiral out of control.'

'So, this man is a big-shot detective or something?' Rajat asked, still incredulous.

'I've heard he's consulted for RAW on a few cases,' Hrishikesh replied. 'Apparently, he has a knack for solving complex problems.'

'What's his name again?'

Before Hrishikesh could answer, a knock at the door interrupted them. A constable entered, looking hesitant. 'Sorry to disturb you, Sir. Some Victor Chatterjee is here to meet you. He says he has an appointment with you. Err… he mentioned you requested it.'

Hrishikesh and Rajat exchanged a stunned glance, the weight of the moment sinking in. The game had just changed.

***

The man who entered the room was quite the opposite of what Rajat had imagined. Victor Chatterjee was a tall, well-built young man dressed casually. He looked more like a sportsman than a professor, his sharp, mind-piercing eyes giving him an air of quiet intensity.

After a brief introduction, Hrishikesh began, 'The Home Minister was quite confident you could help us. Have you been briefed about the case? I guess he called you himself.'

'Nope,' Victor replied calmly. 'The assistant director of RAW, Mr Patkar, called me. I've worked with him before, but he didn't tell me much. I know a bit from the newspapers. He requested that I assist you in arresting this killer and told me you'd brief me.'

'Well, there is a file with all the case findings. You can go through it,' Rajat said curtly.

'Sure, but what is your progress on this case?' Victor asked his tone even.

'Well, I think everyone in the city knows the killer's name and how he looks. I have informers all over the city. It's just a matter of time before he's caught. Frankly, I don't believe we need any help to solve this case,' Rajat shrugged dismissively.

'Great. If you're so confident, shall I leave? Honestly, I don't enjoy getting involved in police affairs,' Victor said with a nonchalant shrug.

Hrishikesh intervened quickly, 'Hold on. Let's work together until the killer is behind bars. We don't want to be on bad terms with the Home Minister. Moreover, arresting the killer isn't our only problem. People are glorifying Mohan and considering him a hero. We need to uncover the true motive behind his killings and show the public that he's not a hero.'

'Yes, I think even arresting Mohan won't solve this problem. There will be protests. Perhaps you have some ideas on how to deal with that?' Rajat said with a smirk.

'I do,' Victor replied, his face impassive.

'Really? We're all ears,' Rajat said, leaning back with a hint of sarcasm.

'Let's spread another rumour—that the one-eyed archer has become a contract killer, murdering these women in exchange for money,' Victor suggested.

'What!' Rajat snapped. 'How can the police release such a statement without proof? People are already tainting the victims' reputations. They'll say their husbands hired the killer because their wives cheated on them.'

'I don't think it's a bad idea,' Hrishikesh said thoughtfully. 'At least Mohan wouldn't be a public hero in everyone's eyes. Some people would believe the contract-killer theory, which might prevent protests after his arrest. But, as Rajat pointed out, we can't make any official statement like this.'

'No need for an official statement,' Victor said. 'I'll make an anonymous post on all the popular messaging apps and forward it to my entire contact list. By evening, the messages will spread across the city, and no one will know where they came from. People crave rumours—let's give them what they want.'

'Could there be any truth to it?' Hrishikesh asked, his tone speculative. 'It seems like a plausible theory.'

Rajat dismissed him instantly, 'I don't think so, Sir. This killer just wants to spread terror. It wouldn't be surprising if he's connected to some cross-border terrorist organization. Otherwise, why is RAW involved? Maybe Victor knows.'

'Wouldn't I have told you if I knew?' Victor retorted. 'Patkar didn't tell me anything other than that you needed my help.'

'Can't you call and ask him?' Rajat inquired.

'Unfortunately, no. The number he calls me from shows as

invalid when dialled. Whenever he needs me, he calls. I can't call him back,' Victor explained.

'What's your plan, Victor? Apart from spreading the contract-killer rumour,' Hrishikesh asked.

'Nothing much. I'll start by going through the case file,' Victor replied.

'Don't you want to visit the murder sites?'

'Sure, once the next murder happens. The previous scenes are already contaminated; visiting them now would be pointless.'

'You mean you're certain there will be more murders?' Hrishikesh asked, leaning forward.

'At least four,' Victor said with conviction.

'Nothing like that will happen,' Rajat snapped. 'I'll catch Mohan soon, and this will be over.'

'You can use your informers to watch for unusual activity in partially built or abandoned buildings,' Victor suggested. 'Though I'm not sure that'll be enough.'

'I'm doing much more than that,' Rajat shot back. 'If Mohan returns, he'll try to meet his parents. My team is already watching his village in plain clothes. Plus, the police and my informers are scouring the city for him. We'll catch him before he strikes again.'

'Good luck with that,' Victor said, rising from his chair. 'But if you fail, I'd like to see the next murder scene uncontaminated.'

***

Rajat became busy as soon as Victor had left. As he had declared proudly in front of the Commissioner, Rajat was determined to arrest Mohan before he could commit another murder. Not only his but the entire department's reputation was at stake.

He first called the team posted at Mohan's village and learned that Mohan had not visited his parents yet. Then he called his informers individually, but no one had helpful information. None of them had spotted Mohan anywhere in the city.

His hopes of salvaging the department's reputation were shattered in the afternoon when he heard that a third murder had occurred in New Town. Reluctantly, he dialled Victor's number after being reminded by the Commissioner as soon as the call came from the crime scene.

Rajat reached the housing complex in New Town within an hour and found Victor waiting at the entrance.

Before Rajat could speak, Victor pointed to a partially built housing complex across the main road, 'Send your men there. I think you'll find the unused arrow.'

'You think the shot was taken from there? Isn't that about three hundred meters from this complex?'

'Yes, an incredible distance. Done possibly only by Mohan. But why do you think he always leaves an arrow at the spot?'

'I believe he keeps an extra arrow as a backup in case he misses the first shot, which never happens. So, he leaves immediately without wasting time to pack the remaining arrow,' Rajat speculated.

Victor mused, 'Maybe. It may also be his signature. I think Mohan wants the world to know about his feat.'

'Show-off!' Rajat smirked. 'His pride will be the end of him one day.'

'Don't be so confident, Officer. You have no idea if, at any moment, an arrow could come flying from nowhere and find your left eye. If he can shoot so accurately from such a distance, he could kill one of us anytime.'

Rajat became alert at this comment and said, 'Let's go inside.'

Victor said, 'I think CCTV monitors this complex. I want to check the footage before going to the crime scene.'

Rajat looked confused, 'Are you sure? What are you expecting to find there? Mohan never entered this complex. Let's go to the building under construction.'

'Yes, later. But first, I want to see who entered and left the apartment from morning until the incident.'

'Well, it's your wish,' Rajat shrugged. 'You can sit here with the building security and check. I'll go to that building from where the arrow was shot. But I'm tight on schedule, so I can't keep that uncontaminated.'

'It's okay. Go ahead,' Victor said. 'If you're going, I don't need to go there.'

After Rajat left with the constable, Victor entered the small security room near the gate and asked for the footage.

The security guard, named Rana, turned out to be very efficient. He said, 'Sir, CCTV cameras are installed on every floor, covering all the apartment entrances. The murder took place in Block B on the fourth floor. I've already checked the CCTV footage of that apartment. Three persons entered the apartment after Ranajoy Sir left in the morning and before Asha Madam's body was found.'

'Great job. Can you show me?'

'Sure, Sir,' Rana said while strolling through the footage.

Rana gave a running commentary. 'Look here. Ranajoy Sir is leaving the house at 10 am sharp. The househelp Molly had been in the house since 9 am. She left at 11 am, closing the door herself from outside. It looks like she was talking to Madam while leaving. Unfortunately, we can't see Madam in the footage because the camera is fitted at one corner, not directly in front of the door. No one entered the apartment for a couple of hours after that. Now, at 12:55 pm, this lady from the beauty parlour came. She made an entry in the register at the gate, too.'

'Okay, but we can't see her face on the CCTV.'

'That's the problem in this building, Sir. They've installed many cameras, but all are fixed at a high level. So, we can't see the face unless someone looks directly at the camera. But as I told you, I saw this lady when she entered the gate. At least she didn't look like a murderer.' Rana chuckled.

'Let's move forward,' Victor said, pointing at the monitor.

'Sure, Sir.' Rana fast-forwarded the clip. 'At around 2 pm, this lady left.'

The footage showed the woman leaving with her trolley bag, closing the door behind her while talking to someone inside, probably bidding adieu. A glimpse of her face was visible this time, but not clear enough.

'After half an hour, this electrician came,' Rana continued.

In the footage, a man wearing a grey uniform appeared at the door. He was carrying a large bag through which a hammer was visible. He rang the doorbell, set the bag on the floor, and started fiddling with his phone as if playing a game. The door opened after a while; the electrician entered and left the door ajar. Asha wasn't visible on camera, but the door was opened from the inside, as the electrician never touched it.

'He left within 15 minutes,' Rana said as the footage showed the man leaving, salaaming someone inside and closing the door behind him.

Victor commented, 'His bag seems heavier than when he entered. Maybe he took something.'

'You mean stole?' Rana frowned.

'Not at all. Perhaps he was given something for repair. Let's move ahead.'

'The next visitor was Molly again at 4 pm. When she came, Madam didn't open the door. Then she called me. After ringing the bell several times, I broke into the apartment and found Madam in such a horrible condition.'

'So, we can talk to these people? The maid, the beautician, and the electrician?'

'Molly is still here. The beautician entered her name as Riya and left a phone number, but I think it's the company's helpline. However, she's been visiting Asha Madam regularly for several months. You might find her number on Madam's phone. The electrician came from the same company. Most dwellers in this complex book services from this company.'

'Yes, I noticed from their uniform.'

'Well, you'll have to call the company to talk to them.'

'That won't be necessary,' a voice said from behind.

Victor turned to see Rajat standing there, 'The arrow was shot from that building. We found the spare arrow, just like the previous spots. So, there's no need to beat around the bushes. Do you want to see the body?'

'Yes, I need to see the apartment as well.'

Rajat frowned and waved his hand. 'Let's go then.'

***

The murder scene was harrowing. Asha, a woman in her early thirties, lay lifeless on the bed. Her body faced an open window through which the under-construction building was visible. A black arrow was impaled in her left eye.

'Same as the previous crime scenes,' Rajat remarked.

Victor remained silent.

Rajat stepped closer to examine the body. 'She seems to be wearing makeup. Perhaps she was planning to go somewhere but didn't make it.'

'A make-up artist named Riya visited her today. I confirmed it on the CCTV,' Victor said.

'So, she must be the last person to see her alive.'

'No, that would be the electrician. You should've checked the footage,' Victor corrected.

'Anyway, it doesn't matter,' Rajat snapped. 'We know where the murder was committed, so whoever saw her last doesn't change anything.'

'Maybe one of them saw something,' Victor suggested.

'Really? If the electrician was the last person to see her alive, wouldn't he have raised an alarm if he noticed anything? The murder must have happened after he left.'

'Hmm,' Victor nodded.

A constable entered the room and whispered something into Rajat's ear. Rajat's expression darkened.

'The victim's husband, Ranajoy Deb, is a prominent politician, and he's causing a scene outside. Do you need to see anything else here? I've got other matters to handle.'

'No, let's go.'

As they returned to the living room, a middle-aged man stormed into the apartment. He wore an impeccably white kurta and pyjama, golden-rimmed spectacles, and an expensive wristwatch. His bloodshot eyes betrayed grief and rage.

'What have you been doing?' he shouted at Rajat. 'You should've arrested or shot this killer long ago. Now my wife...' His voice broke before he blurted, 'Mohan Singh must die, and I'll make sure of it.'

'Don't take the law into your own hands, Mr Deb. You have a reputation. The police are doing their best to apprehend Mohan.'

'You haven't done a damn thing!' Ranajoy yelled. 'If you had, my wife would still be alive. I heard the killer's parents live in a nearby village. Torture them, and they'll talk.'

'We're leaving no stone unturned, I assure you,' Rajat replied firmly.

Victor suddenly asked, 'Mr Deb, could you check if any electronic items are missing from your house? Did you give anything for repair?'

'Excuse me. Who is this man?' Ranajoy asked, turning to Rajat.

'He is… err, a specialist assisting with the investigation,' Rajat replied, hesitating.

'I'm not aware of any such items. Asha managed those things. Frankly, I don't have time for this.'

'I've seen enough here,' Victor said, addressing Rajat. 'See you later.'

As he was leaving, Victor stopped to inspect the door lock. He pressed his thumb repeatedly on the spring latch, pausing to examine it. The door lock was a handle-spring latch mechanism with a deadbolt that required a key. Finally, he remarked, 'The area near the spring latch feels sticky like adhesive was applied.'

He stepped back into the room and bent down to pick up something small from the floor.

'What is it?' Rajat asked.

'A torn piece of nylon thread,' Victor replied, holding it up. 'There's a knot on it.'

'Does this matter to the investigation?' Rajat asked impatiently.

'I'm not sure yet. I'll find out,' With that, Victor left the apartment.

***

Victor visited Mohan's village that evening, driving for an hour and a half from the city. Darkness had already settled when he knocked on the door of Mohan's parents' house. Rajat had given him the address but had shown no interest in accompanying him, dismissing it with, 'They know nothing—I've already interrogated them.'

Mohan's parents, a frail couple in their seventies, lived alone in a modest two-room house. Yet, as Victor glanced at their possessions, he suspected the poverty was a façade—they were far from destitute.

Udham Singh, Mohan's father, was a thin man with a mop of greying hair. He eyed Victor warily and said, 'I've told the police a hundred times—we know nothing about these murders. My son died fifteen years ago. Why can't you people let him rest in peace?'

Victor offered a measured smile, 'I didn't come to ask about Mohan. I'm here to learn about someone who supported him—a man who discovered your son's talent and trained him for the Olympics. His name isn't in the police files. Can you help me find him?'

Udham's expression softened slightly, 'Vikrant Sir. We owe him everything for what he did for Mohan. But why do you need to meet him? Why can't anyone understand—Mohan is gone. He died years ago.'

'I'm not here to ask about Mohan's whereabouts. I need Vikrant's expert opinion. That's all.'

After a long pause, Udham sighed and reached into a drawer. He handed Victor a visiting card, 'Call him, but don't mention my name.'

Victor accepted it with a nod, 'Thank you. I knew you'd help. I'm sorry for the intrusion.'

As Victor turned to leave, four men materialized from the shadows, blocking the door. One of them was Ranajoy Deb, his immaculate attire at odds with the thuggish company he kept.

'Now, now, Mr Specialist,' Ranajoy sneered. 'What are you doing here?'

Victor's tone remained calm, 'I might ask you the same.'

'Well, that's none of your concern. I suggest you leave.'

Victor took a step forward, 'Not before you explain what you're doing here.'

One of Ranajoy's men suddenly lunged at Victor with a punch aimed at his face. Victor evaded the blow effortlessly, moving with the precision of someone who had anticipated the attack. He retaliated with a sharp palm strike to the attacker's jaw, sending him sprawling to the floor. Another thug rushed forward, only to be stopped by a sidekick to the chest that knocked him into a third man. All three ended up in a heap.

'Enough!' Ranajoy barked, pulling a pistol from his pocket and aiming it at Victor. Victor remained unflinching, his gaze steady and unreadable. Being a trained MMA fighter and a Krav Maga expert, he could have easily disarmed and neutralized him in a second. But he made no move, his instincts tempered by the presence of the terrified elderly couple behind him. He couldn't risk their safety.

The first thug staggered to his feet, rage contorting his face as he prepared to attack again. Ranajoy stopped him with a sharp command, 'No more bloodshed. I need an answer to only one question from these old fools. Once I get the answer, I'll leave. The question is straightforward. Where is Mohan?'

'I do not think they know the answer. The police are watching this place. The assistant commissioner will know what you're doing,' Victor said.

'Shut up. I just bribed the constable by 10,000 bucks to take a break. So, no one is watching this place,' Ranajoy smirked.

He gave the gun to one of the thugs and instructed, 'This man makes another move, shoot him.'

Then he turned his attention to Udham, 'Now, old man. Will you tell me where he is?'

'I don't know, Sir,' Udham replied almost in a broken voice.

'Fool. You don't know who you're messing with. Perhaps it's time I make you understand,' Ranajoy raised his hand to slap him, his anger boiling over.

What happened at that moment left even Victor awestruck. A sharp whistle sliced through the air, followed by an arrow piercing Ranajoy's raised palm. He let out a guttural scream and collapsed, clutching his injured hand. The arrow had indeed come through the open door. The thug holding the pistol spun toward the darkness outside, his confusion mirroring the shock etched on everyone's faces.

Victor peeked out but saw nothing—it was pitch black beyond the door. The stillness of the night was broken only by Ranajoy's agonized wails.

The thugs, now visibly panicked, didn't linger. One after another, they bolted into the darkness.

'Don't leave me, you cowards!' Ranajoy shouted after them, his voice hoarse with pain.

Victor knelt beside him, 'Thugs never stick around when things go south. Let me help you. Do you have a car?'

Ranajoy grimaced, clutching his injured hand. 'It's parked outside. But if I go out, he'll kill me.'

'If he wanted to kill you, he would have. Come with me.'

Victor turned to Udham, 'You're safe now. No one will bother you again. Thank you for your help.'

Victor helped Ranajoy to his feet and guided him out to the car. Victor's grip on Ranajoy's arm was firm, a silent assurance that the chaos was under control. 'Let me drive,' he offered. 'I'll take you to a friend—a surgeon. He has a setup for minor surgeries at home.'

'Minor? An arrow is sticking out of my hand! I'll die from the pain,' Ranajoy wailed.

Victor's tone turned sharp, 'You're not dying. The arrow missed any major arteries or veins. Just keep quiet.'

After a few minutes of silence, Ranajoy muttered, 'Why are you helping me? What do you want?'

Victor didn't take his eyes off the road, 'I want you to keep this incident to yourself. If the police ask, say it was an accident.'

'Are you insane? You're helping him! He killed my wife!'

Victor's voice remained steady, 'No, I'm not helping him. But I need to understand a few things before taking any action. Trust me—your wife will get justice. And think about your reputation. If word gets out that you came here like a goon and got injured, what will people think?'

Ranajoy's anger gave way to realization, 'You're right. My party would probably expel me. I… I got carried away. My Asha…'

He broke into sobs.

Victor softened his tone, 'Nothing will happen if you stay quiet. That's why I'm taking you to my friend, not a hospital. But I need one more thing from you.'

'What's that?' Ranajoy asked warily.

Victor pointed to the arrow still lodged in his hand, 'This.'

***

The next morning, Victor made an appointment with the archery coach Vikrant Rout over the phone, using the card he had obtained from Mohan's father. Before heading to the club, he stopped at police headquarters to meet Rajat. As expected,

Rajat was unaware of yesterday evening's development—Ranajoy hadn't filed an official complaint.

Victor asked, 'Can I borrow all of the arrows? I want to show them to a professional archer.'

'Well, you can, but be careful. If you lose them, you'll be charged for tampering with evidence.'

'I'll take utmost care. Please give them in separate bags—the arrows used in the murders and those found in the empty buildings.'

'Sure. By the way, your plan worked. You can check the news. Many people now believe the theory that Mohan is a contract killer. While some still consider him a messiah, there's no agitation in the city so far.'

Victor smiled wryly.

***

Victor reached the Calcutta Archery Club shortly before midday. Coach Vikrant had just finished his morning teaching session and was waiting for Victor in the club room. He was a tall, stout man in his sixties, bald with a thick grey moustache.

He greeted Victor, 'How can I help you?'

Victor said, 'As I mentioned over the phone, I'm assisting the police with the recent murders. I'd like you to examine these arrows.' Victor opened his bag and revealed two sets of arrows, each stored in transparent plastic bags. 'The arrows in the left-side bag were used in the murders, and these were found in the nearby empty buildings.'

'Can I take them out?'

'Sure, but please wear these gloves.' Victor handed him a pair of nitrile gloves from his pocket.

Vikrant sifted through both sets, his expression growing serious. 'Very curious,' he muttered.

Victor leaned in. 'Can you explain?'

'Look at the fletchings at the back of the arrows. We can also call them vanes. These help the arrows cut through the air and reach their target precisely. Each arrow has three fletchings, one of which is an odd colour. For instance, two vanes are blue, and the third is white. Let me show you something.'

The clubhouse was immaculate, with a large oval centre table holding a platter of fruit, a tray of cupcakes and biscuits, and a coffee machine. Comfortable couches surrounded the table, and the walls were adorned with various types of bows and arrows.

Vikrant took a bow from the wall. 'This is a recurve bow. Now give me one of these arrows.'

Victor handed him one of the murder weapons. Vikrant attached it to the bowstring. 'Notice how the odd-colour vane faces left. This indicates it's properly fletched for a recurve bow. Now, let's try another.'

He picked an arrow from the other set, attached it to the bowstring, and said, 'Here, the odd-colour vane faces upward. This one is adjusted for a compound bow and won't work properly with a recurve bow unless I adjust it.'

He rotated the nock point at the back of the arrow, aligning the white vane to the left, 'Now it's suitable for a recurve bow.'

Victor's brow furrowed. 'So, there are two types of arrows here, meant for different kinds of bows?'

'Exactly. They're from the same set—carbon arrows of the same make—but some are adjusted for recurve bows and others for compound bows. As you saw, they can be re-adjusted easily.'

'Why would someone carry two types of arrows?'

'Compound bows are more accurate over long distances.'

'And Mohan? Which bow would he prefer?'

Vikrant's face darkened, 'I don't believe Mohan is capable of such heinous acts. Moreover, we don't even know if he's alive.'

'Mohan committed four murders fifteen years ago,' Victor reminded him.

'That was different. Those people ruined his life. But killing innocent women…'

Victor pressed, 'Does that justify murder?'

Vikrant remained silent.

Victor repeated, 'What bow would Mohan prefer?'

'Recurve. He didn't like compound bows—said they were too easy.'

'But could he shoot well with a compound bow?'

'Better than anyone else I knew. But he could shoot equally well with a recurve bow, regardless of distance.'

'He used a recurve bow for those murders?' Victor asked.

'Yes, that's what I've heard. He didn't have the money for two bows and used the ones at the club. I gifted him the recurve bow when he was preparing for the Olympics.'

'One last thing before I leave.' Victor opened his bag and revealed the arrow that had pierced Ranajoy's palm. 'Have a look at this.'

Vikrant examined it closely. 'This is a crossbow arrow. It's shorter and has a different groove at the back. Also, it's a composite arrow with an alloy core and a carbon coating—high quality and expensive.'

'Are crossbows more accurate?'

'Absolutely. They're as precise as sniper rifles. But where did you get this arrow?'

'I believe Mohan shot it.'

Vikrant shook his head, 'Strange. Crossbows are usually

used for hunting or by the military for stealth killing. How could Mohan afford such expensive equipment? There must be a mistake.'

Victor chuckled, 'Mohan may not be as poor as you think.'

***

Victor received a call from the Police Commissioner in the afternoon. Hrishikesh's voice carried a note of despair.

'There's been another murder, Victor. This time, the victim is the famous actress Priya Jha. Rajat didn't want to inform you—he thinks you're not helping anyway. But he's at his wit's end, and so am I. We need all hands on deck right now. Both the central and state governments are pressuring us heavily. If these murders continue, we'll have no choice but to impose a curfew in the city,' Hrishikesh sighed audibly.

'That won't be necessary,' Victor said nonchalantly. 'I don't think there'll be another murder.'

'How can you be so sure?' Hrishikesh asked, his disbelief evident. 'Just because only four people were killed fifteen years ago doesn't mean it'll stop here. We can't afford to take chances. If we don't catch Mohan soon, he might start another cycle of murders in the future.'

'You can relax. The killer will be caught tonight or tomorrow at the latest,' Victor replied with quiet confidence.

'You're serious?' Hrishikesh asked, momentarily stunned. 'You know where to find him?'

'I have my suspicions. I just need to confirm a few things first. I'll let you know once I've cleared up the confusion.'

Hrishikesh exhaled, a glimmer of hope in his tone. 'That would be a relief. Do you want to visit the murder scene? I can inform Rajat that you'll be joining him.'

'I'll be there shortly,' Victor assured him before ending the call.

***

Victor reached the housing complex where the fourth murder had taken place. It was a luxurious complex with towering, multi-storied buildings that only the affluent could afford. Some towers were still under construction, as the complex was relatively new. At the front gate, two police constables struggled to keep journalists and grieving fans at bay as Victor made his way through.

Rajat stood near the playground, his expression grim. Though displeased by Victor's presence, he refrained from voicing any complaints.

He asked, 'Do you want to see the body? This is a high-profile case. We must move it quickly—the media is already creating chaos outside.'

'No, I don't need to. You can move the body. But I do need to speak to the bereaved family.'

'Yes, you can talk to her husband.'

'Was anyone else living in the house?'

'No. Her husband was her only family. The couple didn't have any kids. Her parents died in a car crash when she was 15, and she was their only child.'

'This is the tower she lived in?' Victor pointed to the block Rajat was facing.

'Yes, that's the one. See the open window on the eleventh floor? The body was found in front of it—the same as the previous victims. The shot was taken from that tower over there, on the thirteenth floor.' Rajat gestured toward a nearby under-construction tower. 'We found the spare arrow and arrow case there, as usual.'

'Almost 200 metres,' Victor murmured, his gaze narrowing as he calculated the distance.

'Also, for your information,' Rajat continued, 'I checked the CCTV footage. Priya's husband, Nishant, left for work at 9 am. No one visited the apartment all day. When the househelp arrived at 4 pm and couldn't get in, she called security. After repeated calls to Priya went unanswered, the security team broke in and discovered the body. According to the forensic team, she had been dead for 4–6 hours—rigor mortis had fully developed. She was still in her nightdress. Nishant said she was sleeping when he left the apartment. She usually got up at 10 am, so I assume she was killed between 10 and 11.'

'When did Nishant return?'

'He was in his studio when security called and informed him about the incident. He rushed here immediately.'

'Studio?'

'Oh, it seems you know nothing about the film industry. Nishant was Priya's makeup artist before they fell in love and got married. He comes from a middle-class family—his father was a police constable who worked under Hrishikesh Sir. Today, Nishant owns the largest and most popular makeup studio in the city. Probably, his millionaire wife contributed generously.'

'He must be in shock. Will he talk to me?'

'He's surprisingly calm. I was taken aback. If I had a golden goose like Priya, I'd be shattered to lose her.' Rajat chuckled, though his tone carried a hint of cynicism.

***

Nishant Jha was a handsome man in his thirties. Though not very tall, his slim physique and suave appearance exuded charm. It wasn't hard to see why Priya had fallen for him.

Victor and Rajat sat with him in his spacious, meticulously decorated living room. Despite Nishant's composed demeanour, grief was etched into his features.

Victor introduced himself as a specialist assisting the police, 'I may ask some personal questions that might not seem directly related to the case,' he said, his tone measured. 'But trust me, they are important.'

Nishant gave him an odd look but nodded.

Victor began, 'How long were you married?'

'Two years,' Nishant replied.

'You were her makeup artist before that?'

'Not just Priya's. I've been in the industry for seven years and have worked with many prominent actors.'

'I hear you own the largest makeup studio in the city.'

'Priya dreamed of me becoming a successful businessman. She always supported me.'

'Supported you financially as well?'

Nishant's expression briefly hardened, but he quickly regained composure, 'Yes.'

'With her passing, I assume you inherit her fortune. Will you be the sole owner now?'

'Excuse me!' Nishant's voice trembled with anger. 'Do you have any idea how painful it is to lose the person you love most? You could at least show some sympathy. Her money is the last thing on my mind right now.'

Victor's gaze remained steady, 'So it's on your mind, even if it's the last thing.'

'Enough!' Nishant stood abruptly, his voice breaking, 'I can't talk to you anymore. I don't care who you are or what you do. My world is shattered, and I won't tolerate this humiliation—not today.'

He stormed into his bedroom and shut the door behind him.

Rajat looked at Victor, dumbfounded, 'Why did you do that? I joked about him earlier but didn't expect you to go this far. It was a mistake letting you talk to him. I don't need your help anymore. You can leave.'

Victor stood and said calmly, 'I'll go. But I need to tell you something important first. Could you step outside with me?'

Rajat hesitated, visibly displeased, but something in Victor's tone compelled him to comply.

'What is it?' he asked as they entered the elevator.

Victor turned to him, 'Do you really think Nishant is as innocent as he seems? He's just hit the jackpot with Priya's death.'

Rajat frowned, 'What's your point? We know who the killer is. Shouldn't we focus all our efforts on catching Mohan?'

Victor's voice remained calm, 'And how has that been working out? Despite all your resources, have you found a single trace of him?'

Rajat sighed, frustration creeping into his tone, 'You're right. He's always one step ahead. I'm out of ideas. What do you suggest?'

'You remember the rumour we spread to prevent unrest? Let's explore that angle further.'

Rajat raised an eyebrow, 'You think these husbands hired Mohan to kill their wives? Do you have any proof?'

'No, because we haven't looked in that direction yet. But if we get one of them to confess, we might learn how to contact Mohan. Then, we can set a trap for him. Maybe you could pretend to hire him yourself.' Victor smirked, 'You could say your wife is causing you trouble.'

'I'm not married,' Rajat replied, clearing his throat. 'But how do we get a confession from any of them?'

Victor leaned in slightly, 'One of them might have left a clue—maybe a scrap of paper with a phone number. Not at home; they'd know the police would search there. But they wouldn't expect us to check their workplaces. For instance, the first victim's husband works in an office—it would take a lot of paperwork to get a search warrant. The second husband is abroad, and the third is politically untouchable without solid proof. But this fourth man, Nishant, is our key. He owns a large studio and likely has a private room there. He might have left something behind—enough to make him talk. If we don't find anything there, you'll have to get warrants for Barun Sen's office and Ranajoy Deb's party headquarters tomorrow.'

Rajat considered this, 'If we catch Mohan using Nishant as bait, we might uncover who hired him for the other murders. But it's a long shot.'

'Have a better idea?' Victor challenged.

Rajat grimaced, 'No. But searching Nishant's studio will be like finding a needle in a haystack. What are we even looking for?'

Victor's eyes gleamed, 'First, find out what time the studio closes tonight. Then, after it's closed, call Nishant and tell him we need to search it as part of the investigation. Say you have a warrant and will begin the search early tomorrow morning. If he's hidden anything, he'll try to remove it tonight.'

Rajat stared at him, incredulous, 'That's straight out of a detective novel. You seriously think he'll fall for this bullshit?'

'Yes,' Victor said, his smirk widening. 'This kind of bullshit always works.'

***

It was 11 o'clock at night when Victor's car pulled into a parking lot opposite Nishant's studio. Rajat sat beside him, dressed in plain clothes. A police vehicle waited a short distance away, ready to act at a moment's notice. The parking lot, with at least thirty cars scattered around, provided enough cover for them to stay hidden while keeping a clear view of the studio.

The studio was a sleek, three-storied building with glass façades that gleamed faintly under the streetlights. A glowing neon sign in front of the building read 'Glam and Glow.' At this hour, the front door was locked, and the building was cloaked in darkness.

Victor and Rajat stepped out of the car after a while to stretch their legs.

'I don't know if this is an utter waste of time,' Rajat muttered, fishing out a packet of cigarettes from his pocket.

'Can you please not smoke now? I can't stand the smell,' Victor said, frowning.

'Oh, come on. I'm bored and still don't know why I'm here.'

Victor pulled out a packet of chewing gum from his jacket. 'Take this instead. And trust me, we're not wasting time. He'll come. Wait… a car just pulled over there.'

A black sedan slowed to a halt across the street, a block away from the studio. A figure emerged, clad in a black hoodie and jeans, and moved toward the studio.

'He didn't even wait till midnight! He has surely left some evidence here and got panicked by my call. Let's move,' Rajat suddenly sounded excited.

'Wait till he enters. Otherwise, he may see us.'

The man in the hoodie didn't use the front door to enter the studio. Instead, he vanished in the dark alley between the studio and the building beside it.

'There is a back entrance. Let's move. Call your team also.' Victor said.

Victor and Rajat crossed the road and entered the alley. They found a doorway leading into the building, which was left ajar.

'Gun ready,' Victor whispered.

Rajat nodded, drawing his weapon.

The building was shrouded in darkness, with faint streaks of streetlight filtering through the glass windows, casting enough illumination to navigate without stumbling. The ground floor featured a spacious waiting area and several cubicles, but it was utterly deserted.

Victor gestured toward the staircase. They climbed silently, their footsteps muffled on the steps. The first floor was equally empty, housing a smaller waiting area and several closed rooms.

A faint sound—muffled footsteps—echoed above, breaking the stillness. Victor pointed upward, and they continued their cautious ascent.

The top floor consisted mainly of office rooms and VIP suites. At the far end of the corridor, light spilled out from beneath a door. The faint noise of objects being moved confirmed someone's presence inside. Victor and Rajat advanced silently.

The room appeared to be a storage area with a narrow door, a key still inserted in the doorknob. Through the small rectangular glass panel, they could see Nishant. His hoodie was pushed back, revealing his face, as he finished packing a large duffel bag, seemingly preparing to leave.

Victor and Rajat burst into the room, catching Nishant off guard. Rajat stepped forward, his gun levelled, and barked, 'Drop the bag and put your hands up. Now! Good. Move away from it—slowly. To the corner. No sudden moves.'

Nishant's face contorted with rage; his burning eyes locked on Rajat. But under the barrel of the gun, he had no choice but to comply.

Victor's steady voice said, 'Your team must be here now. Call them. He might try something desperate, knowing the trouble he's in.'

Rajat relayed the order through his walkie-talkie. Within moments, footsteps echoed from the stairwell, and two constables entered the room, quickly handcuffing Nishant.

'Take him to the van,' Rajat ordered, his tone sharp.

'Wait,' Victor interjected, holding up a hand. 'Let him watch while I open the bag.'

Rajat hesitated but nodded.

Victor opened the duffel bag, glanced inside, and a sly grin crept across his face.

'I didn't expect to find this here. I thought you'd have disposed of it by now. I suppose you never anticipated the police coming here, did you?'

Victor took a hefty toy car from the bag, followed by a cell phone.

Rajat frowned, 'What is this junk?'

'I'll tell you later. The more intriguing revelations are yet to come,' Victor said with amusement.

Reaching into the bag, Victor pulled out a heavy object—a black half-bust human figure made entirely of solid rubber. He carefully placed it on top of a large cardboard box. The rubber model was riddled with small punctures, most of them concentrated around the left eye.

Rajat stared, visibly perplexed. 'I don't understand any of this.'

Victor's expression remained calm. 'Wait. The real shock is

coming.'

This time, Victor retrieved a set of arrows from the bag—four of them—identical to the ones used in the murders. Rajat's face paled as the realization struck.

'My God!' he exclaimed. 'This proves Nishant hired Mohan and supplied the arrows to him.'

Victor shook his head, incredulous. 'Are you truly this gullible? Even now, you believe Mohan did this? Mohan likely died fifteen years ago and never returned. This,' Victor pointed directly at Nishant, his fiery gaze unwavering, 'is your killer.'

'What?! Are you saying Nishant is as skilled an archer as Mohan? That's impossible! Have you lost your mind?' Rajat's voice rose in disbelief.

'Who ever said Nishant is an archer? This man wouldn't know how to string a bow,' Victor countered coldly.

'Then what the hell are you suggesting? How did he murder those women?' Rajat demanded.

Victor grasped one of the arrows, gripping it firmly at a point one-third from its tip. In a swift, precise motion, he drove it into the rubber model's left eye. The arrow pierced cleanly through, its sharp tip emerging from the back of the head.

'This,' Victor said, his voice laced with finality, 'is how he killed them.'

***

The next morning, Victor again found himself seated in the Police Commissioner's office. Unlike Rajat, who sat beside him with bleary eyes after a long night of filing reports, Victor had gone straight home after the raid and enjoyed a good night's sleep.

Hrishikesh's voice carried a tone of urgency as he addressed them. 'Even though we know who the murderer is, there are still many unanswered questions. I'm sorry to call you so early, but we have a press conference in a few hours.'

Victor, sipping his coffee, replied, 'Let me explain things in my way. If you have any questions afterwards, feel free to ask. By the way, has Nishant made any statements?'

Rajat shook his head. 'He's... refusing to talk, asking for his lawyer. But that won't help him. We caught him red-handed with all his tools.'

Victor's tone was calm and measured as he began, 'The human mind tends to believe in the impossible. To deceive it, you only need to deceive the eyes. There were glaring oddities in this case from the beginning, but none of us noticed them because we were enthralled by the legend of the one-eyed archer. I went through the case file you gave me and reviewed the murders from 15 years ago. Interestingly, nowhere was it explicitly stated that all those murders were committed from long distances. Only the minister's assassination was from approximately 200 meters away. The distances for the other murders were unknown.'

He leaned forward slightly, his eyes narrowing. 'Now compare that with the empty buildings where we found the spare arrows in these recent cases. All of them were over 200 meters away. I'm not underestimating Mohan's abilities. He may have been one of the best archers in the world, but even he wasn't a comic-book superhero. It's improbable, even for someone of his skill, to maintain 100 per cent accuracy at such distances every time. He likely got lucky with the minister, while the other murders were executed from much shorter ranges, with Mohan remaining hidden. However, the public turned him into a mythological figure. Even if we accept that Mohan could make precise long-distance shots, how did he consistently find homemakers alone in their homes for four consecutive murders? Isn't that far too much of a coincidence? These are the glaring facts we chose to ignore just because we love myths.'

Hrishikesh interjected, 'When did you start piecing this together?'

Victor took another sip of coffee before answering. 'After visiting the third crime scene. There, I picked up on small clues that began to unravel the bigger picture. But let me start from the beginning.'

After a brief pause, he continued, 'The first thing that struck me as odd was the abundance of evidence pointing to Mohan. Shooting victims in the left eye alone would have been enough to resurrect the legend of the one-eyed archer. Why was it necessary to leave arrows in nearby empty buildings or fabricate alleged sightings of a man with a facial scar and an eye prosthesis? When I read Rajat's case files on the first two murders, these peculiarities stood out. But like everyone else, I was initially blinded by the myth. I thought Mohan might be trying to declare his return with impossible long-range kills, perhaps using some advanced sighting equipment.'

He leaned back, his tone more reflective, 'The turning point came during the investigation of the third murder. The CCTV footage from outside the apartment initially appeared mundane but had one curious detail: why did everyone leaving the apartment close the door themselves from outside? It made sense for the househelp, who was a regular visitor, but it struck me as odd for others.'

Victor's eyes sharpened. 'I found two additional clues inside the apartment: a piece of nylon thread and stickiness on the door lock near the spring latch. These might seem like minor details, but with an open mind, they reveal a lot. When you get home today, take a look at your door lock. Modern spring latch mechanisms are typically very smooth. With a little effort, you can push the spring latch inside and prevent it from snapping back into place by applying adhesive tape. This keeps the door unlocked even if it's closed from the outside, explaining the stickiness I noticed on the lock. As for the nylon thread, I found it near the door and deduced that it was likely tied to the handle and connected to something sturdy—possibly a toy car—to remotely open the door from outside. Then, I recalled the electrician seen in the footage. He was on his mobile phone after knocking on the door, likely controlling the toy car remotely to execute the setup.'

Rajat interrupted, his tone incredulous, 'So, Nishant disguised himself as a beautician, finished Asha's makeup, and killed her with an arrow to the left eye. Then, he tied the nylon thread to the door handle and connected it to the toy car. Before leaving, he pushed the spring latch in and taped it to keep the door unlocked. Later, he returned as an electrician, used the toy car to reopen the door, removed evidence, and left. But why go to such lengths? Why return as an electrician?'

Victor nodded. 'Well, I think he was afraid that the forensic team may match the time of death with the time of the beautician's visit. He also committed the first two murders, visiting as a beautician. Rajat, you mentioned in your note about a male beautician visiting the first victim, which was informed to you by one of the inhabitants. You were disgusted by the allegation about her character but did not forget to write the details in the case file. Nishanth feared someone would connect all the murders with the beautician's visit. So, he returned as an electrician to prove that Asha was still alive when the beautician left. It would have been safer for him to choose an apartment that didn't have CCTV, but I think he could only find two of those.'

Hrishikesh said, 'But I still don't understand how the victims never suspected anything. Sure, hiding an arrow inside a long makeup box is plausible. The victims would have been lying there, eyes closed, trusting him while he killed them. But how did he select his targets so precisely? How did he ensure they'd be alone? And how could he guarantee there would always be an empty building nearby for planting false evidence? Moreover, it seems unlikely that any woman would allow a male beautician into her house when she was alone. So how exactly did he manage all of this?'

Victor chuckled, 'You're still looking for random connections. Nishant left nothing to chance. This was a meticulously crafted plan, months in the making. He wasn't just a beautician—he was dating these women.'

'What?' Rajat exclaimed.

Victor explained, 'Nishant used his charm and charisma to win over women, much like he did with Priya. It's likely he connected with many married women through dating apps, enticing them into romantic or physical relationships. That's how he gained access to their homes. Over several months, he built relationships with these women and eventually selected his three victims. A key criterion for choosing them was the proximity of an under-construction building, which would serve his plan.'

'Now things are starting to make sense,' Hrishikesh sighed. 'But we still need to understand his motive. That will probably come from Nishant's statement.'

'I believe it ties back to his relationship with his wife and her wealth. Among the four husbands, only he stood to benefit from his wife's death. Rajat described Priya as his 'golden goose,' which was likely true when she initially financed Nishant's studio. However, it seems their relationship soured over time and was likely headed for divorce. In such a scenario, Nishant knew he stood to lose everything, including the studio. I suspect he also discovered Priya's infidelity, which might have fuelled his actions and led him to reciprocate with other women. Of course, we'll know the full story when Nishant finally gives his statement.'

Victor sipped his coffee and continued, 'In my opinion, there are three main types of serial killers. The first category is the novel serial killers, like Jack the Ripper or Zodiac. They are deeply disturbed individuals, often driven by their warped logic or ideology. The second category is the copycat serial killers, commonly depicted in Hollywood movies. These individuals are usually mentally unstable but lack originality, emulating others' methods without much creativity. The third category is the fake serial killers. They commit multiple murders to mask their real motive, which is often tied to a single victim. This tactic has been seen in both real life and fiction. However, Nishant introduced a new subcategory: the fake copycat serial killer. He understood that if his wife's death appeared unnatural, suspicion would inevitably fall on him. The only way to deflect attention was to exploit the legend of the one-eyed archer. He must have learned about the legend from his father, who worked under you as a police constable,' Victor said, looking directly at Hrishikesh.

'My God,' Hrishikesh murmured, his voice tinged with disbelief.

Victor continued, 'Once the victims were selected, Nishant purchased the arrows. He had no knowledge of archery, which became evident when I showed the arrows to Mohan's coach. The coach pointed out that the arrows were adjusted for two different types of bows, something that made no sense. While the coach provided a plausible explanation for this, it was clear to me that the murders were committed by someone unfamiliar with archery.

Mohan, an expert, would never have made such an error.

'Had Nishant purchased the arrows from a professional store, they would have been adjusted correctly for the intended bow. However, that would have left a paper trail directly linking him to the murders. Instead, he opted to buy cheap arrows from an online store. These stores prioritize profit over quality and don't bother with adjustments for specific bows.

'Next came the matter of practice. Even though stabbing an arrow into the left eye of a stationary victim lying with their eyes closed might seem straightforward, it still requires precision. Nishant practised extensively in his studio using the rubber dummy we discovered. Arrows are typically sold in sets of six or twelve. Nishant purchased a dozen—eight were used in his plan, while four were reserved for practice. This explains why he didn't dispose of the unused arrows earlier. He needed them for preparation before each murder and likely assumed his studio wouldn't be searched.

'As for records, I'm certain he was careful to cover his tracks. He likely asked the women to delete their chat histories to avoid detection by their husbands. To further obscure his activities, he probably used internet-based calling apps, ensuring there were no traces in conventional call logs.

'Regarding the locations, the first two buildings had no CCTV cameras, which worked in his favour. The third location, however, had cameras, so he tactically managed the situation to avoid suspicion. While it would have been possible to check the road cameras near the murder scenes for parked vehicles, that would've been a long shot. Still, it's evident that a vehicle must have been involved in all these incidents. For the first two murders, he had to wear Mohan's disguise, create a witness, remove the disguise, and then enter the houses to commit the crimes. You already know how he altered his appearance for the third case.'

Victor paused and then asked, 'Any other questions?'

Rajat sighed, 'Why didn't you tell me all this before the raid? You clearly knew everything,'

Victor scoffed lightly. 'Honestly, I wasn't sure you'd believe me, given your scepticism earlier. Plus, we didn't have enough time to go into all the details before the raid.'

Hrishikesh added, 'We're grateful for your help, Victor. But I still don't understand why RAW got involved.'

Victor's expression darkened slightly, 'Even I don't know. Mr Patkar is a mysterious man. He only shares what's necessary for the task at hand, never explaining the bigger picture. If there's nothing else, I'll take my leave.'

All three men stood and shook hands. Rajat walked Victor out. As Victor was about to get into his car, Rajat said, 'I'm sorry for doubting you. I hope we can work together again. Can I call you for help with a future case?'

Victor smiled, 'Make sure it's an interesting one.'

***

Rajat called Victor in the evening and said, 'Nishant has confessed everything.'

'What did he say his motive was?' Victor asked.

'Exactly what you suspected. Their relationship was falling apart. Within a few months of marriage, Priya lost interest in Nishant. She started seeing other men, and Nishant found out. On top of that, she often misbehaved with him and threatened him with divorce. It gets worse—Priya didn't even gift him the studio. She loaned him the money, forcing him to mortgage his parental house as collateral. If they had divorced, Nishant would've lost everything,' Rajat sighed heavily.

Victor listened in silence. As soon as he hung up, his phone rang again. This time, it was Ranajoy Deb.

'Thanks for bringing my wife's killer to justice,' Ranajoy said. 'I'll ensure he pays for what he's done. I heard from the assistant commissioner how brilliantly you solved this case.'

'Thanks,' Victor replied, his tone neutral. 'How's your hand?'

Ranajoy chuckled dryly. 'Ah, about that. You still don't know who shot me, do you?'

Victor's brows furrowed, 'Hmm.'

'I got a call from your friend at RAW—Mr Patkar. Turns out it was his sniper protecting you that night. The sniper mistook my actions as a threat to you. Mr Patkar offered me a hefty compensation package, including the cost of my treatment, in exchange for my silence.'

'And you accepted?'

'I didn't have a choice,' Ranajoy admitted bitterly. 'The other option was prison. The sniper recorded footage of us entering the house armed and attacking you.'

'I see,' Victor said coldly, 'I hope you've learned your lesson.'

As the call ended, Victor placed the phone on his desk and stared at the short crossbow arrow on his study table.

***

Later that evening, Victor stood by the window, gazing into the dark expanse beyond, his thoughts entangled in the intricate threads of the case.

A sharp thud broke his reverie.

Victor flinched slightly, turning to see an arrow embedded in the wooden frame of his window. It was identical to the crossbow arrow on his desk. He immediately scanned the darkness outside but saw no one—only the quiet emptiness of the night.

Returning to the arrow, he noticed something peculiar. A small piece of paper was rolled around the shaft and secured with tape. Carefully, Victor removed the arrow from the window frame and unwrapped the note.

Two words stared back at him, written in a neat hand: 'Thank you.'

Victor stared at the note for a long moment. Then, a faint smile crossed his face as he turned back to the window, his gaze steady and unyielding.

Acknowledgments

Writing Deadly Clues has been a journey filled with mystery, intrigue, and the relentless pursuit of truth—just like the best detective stories.

I extend my deepest gratitude to Srishti Publishers for believing in this book and bringing it to life. A heartfelt thanks to my literary agent, Mr Suhail Mathur, and the incredible team at The Book Bakers, whose unwavering support and tireless efforts made this publication possible.

To my family and friends—your constant encouragement has been my strongest motivation.

And most importantly, to you—the readers. Your passion for crime fiction and detective stories keeps this genre alive. I invite you to step into Victor Chatterjee's world, follow the clues, and solve the mysteries alongside him.

Let's keep the thrill of deduction alive—share your theories, discuss your favourite moments, and become part of the mystery-solving community.

The game is afoot!